"ANOTHER BULLSEYE FOR HIG-GINS!"

The New York Times

"Higgins has a gift for big-city, nether-world smart talk. It is profane and salty, but vigorous and imaginative and full of humor . . . He makes the dialogue do everything but climb up a rope. It reveals character, advances the plot, exposes the past."

Los Angeles Times

"MR. HIGGINS IS A TIGHT, RE-LENTLESS WRITER . . . PURE PLEASURE."

The New Yorker

GEORGE V. HIGGINS
THE DIGGER'S GAME

THE DIGGER'S GAME

George V. Higgins

BALLANTINE BOOKS • NEW YORK

All rights reserved under International and Pan-American Copyright Conventions. Published in the United States by Ballantine Books, a division of Random House, Inc., New York, and simultaneously in Canada by Random House of Canada, Limited, Toronto, Canada.

Library of Congress Catalog Card Number: 72-10417

ISBN 0-345-28970-6

This edition published by arrangement with Alfred A. Knopf, Inc.

Manufactured in the United States of America

First Ballantine Books Edition: February 1981

THERE WERE THREE KEYS on the transmission hump of the XK-E. The driver touched the one nearest the gearshift boot. The fat man, cramped in the passenger bucket, squinted at it in the moonlight.

"Back door," the driver said. "Three steps, aluminum railing, no outer door. No alarm. You got a problem of being seen. There's a whole mess of apartments back up on the place, and they got mostly kids in them and them fucking bastards never go to bed, it seems like. What can I tell you, except be careful."

"Look," the fat man said, "I'm gonna act like I was minding my own business. This is what you say it is, tomorrow morning nobody's even gonna know I was there. Nobody'll remember anything."

"Uh huh," the driver said, "but that's tomorrow. First you got to get through tonight. It's tonight I'd be worried about, I was you."

"I'll decide what I'm gonna worry about," the fat man said.

"You got gloves?" the driver said.

"I don't like gloves," the fat man said. "In this weather especially, I don't like gloves. What the hell, somebody spots me, the heat comes, I'm dead anyway. Gloves ain't gonna help me. You wait like you say you're gonna, nobody's even gonna know I was in there until everybody's been around handling things and so forth."

"That's what I thought," the driver said, "no gloves. I heard that about you. The Digger goes in bare-ass." The driver pulled a pair of black vinyl gloves out of the map pocket on his door. "Wear these."

The Digger took the gloves in his left hand. "Whatever you say, my friend. It's your job." He put the gloves in his lap.

"No," the driver said, "I really mean it, Dig. You want to go in bare-ass, you go in bare-ass. That's all right with me. But you get to that paper, the actual paper, you put them gloves on first, and you keep them on, okay?"

"I wouldn't think it'd help them," the Digger said. "So many people handling the stuff and all. I wouldn't think it'd make much difference, time they found out."

"Well, take my word for it," the driver said, "it does. It really does. Now I really mean it, you know? This is for my protection. Gloves on as soon as you get to the paper."

"Gloves on," the Digger said.

"You get inside," the driver said, "you go left down the corridor and it's the fourth door. The fourth door. There's about six doors in there and they all got the company name on them, but this is for the fourth door." He touched the second key. "It says 'General Manager' down at the bottom, there, so in case you get screwed up, that's the one you're looking for."

"Can I use a light?" the Digger said.

"Not unless you really have to," the driver said. "Near as I can make out, there's no windows anybody can look in and see you moving around, but you never know what'll reflect off something. I was you, unless I absolutely had to, I wouldn't."

"Okay," the Digger said, "no light."

"I don't think you're gonna need one anyway," the driver said. "We got a pretty good moon here and all. You should be able to get along all right."

"Fourth door," the Digger said. "Must be some kind of suspicious outfit, got a different key for every door and all. They must be afraid somebody's gonna come in after hours or something and steal something."

"Well," the driver said, "I don't know that for sure. It could be, this'll open any door, once you get inside.

But the offices're separate, you know? They haven't got any doors between them. So it's not gonna do you any good, you get into the third floor or something, because what we want isn't in there. I'm just trying to save you time, is all."

The driver touched the third key. It was smaller than the first two. "ADT," he said. "Metal box right behind the door, just about eye level. The lock's on the bottom on the right. It's got the yellow monitor light, so you won't have no trouble finding it anyway. Twenty-second delay before it rings. Plenty of time. Oh, sometimes they forget to set it when they lock up. If the yellow light's off, don't touch it. You do and you'll turn it on and then you're gonna have all kinds of company. I'm pretty sure it's on. So you turn it off. I told him, I said, 'Make sure that alarm's on. I don't want nobody coming in Monday and seeing the alarm's off and looking around.' He said he would. But just to be on the safe side, don't touch it if the light isn't on."

"Do I still go in if it's off?" the Digger said.

"Sure," the driver said. "The important thing is, get the paper. I'm just saying, it'd be better if the alarm was on when you go in. And you shut it off and get what we want and then turn it on again and get out. You got another twenty seconds when you turn it on. Oh, and it's a cheapie. No puncher for when it's on and off, no signal anywhere it got turned off. Single stage, it all works off the key. If it's on, and you don't turn it off, it rings. But that's all it does."

"Chickenshit outfit," the Digger said.

"Well," the driver said, "it's really just for the type-writers and, you know, in case the junkies come in and start tearing the place apart. They don't keep any real dough there. It's just for intruders, is all."

"Trespassers," the Digger said.

"Yeah," the driver said, "trespassers. Speaking of which, I assume you're not a shitter or anything."

"No," the Digger said.

"You *know* you're not a shitter, too, don't you?" the driver said.

"Well, I'm pretty sure," the Digger said. "I never

3

done much of this, but when I been in some place, I never did, no."

"Well, in case you get the urge," the driver said, "wait till you get home or something. I had a real good guy that I always used, and he was all right. He could get in any place. You could send him down the Cathedral and he'd steal the cups at High Mass. But Jesus, I used him probably six or seven years and I never have the slightest problem with him, and the next thing I know, he's into some museum or something they got out there to Salem, and he's after silver, you know? And he shits, he turned into a shitter. Left himself a big fuckin' pile of shit right on the goddamned Oriental rug. Well, he wasn't working for me or anything, and hell, everybody in the world was gonna know the next day he was in there, because the silver was gone. But that was the end of him as far as I was concerned, I didn't have no more use for him. The thing is you don't want nobody to know you been in there until you're ready, okay? So no shit on the desks or anything. Keep your pants on.

"The stuff we want," the driver said, "you go over to the file cabinets and they keep them in the third one from the window. The middle drawer, okay? In the back, behind the ledgers. They keep the ledgers up to the front, and then there's the divider there, and the books're behind the divider. There's three of them. The one they're actually using's on top and then there's two more, the reserve ones."

"You got a key for the cabinet?" the Digger said.

"Usually not locked," the driver said. "If it's locked, the key's on the frame of the door you just came through. Up on the wood there, over the door. But's it's probably not gonna be locked. If it's locked, unlock it and then when you're through, lock it again and put the key back. If it's not locked, just open it and take the stuff and then close it up again. Okay?"

"Okay," the Digger said. "You want some canceled checks, I assume."

"Don't need them," the driver said. "Somebody might go looking for something and then they notice they're gone. I got a way, I got something I can copy all ready."

"They don't use a check-signer or anything?" the Digger said.

"Sometimes they do," the driver said, "sometimes they don't. It's got a meter on it and they're pretty careful about that anyway. It's only when the guy's away they use that, and I guess they must've had some trouble or something because they keep that locked up pretty good and it's in another one of them offices, in a safe. So I'm not gonna bother with trying to get that."

"Okay," the Digger said.

"Take from the first book," the driver said. "They're all numbered in sequence and they're about, they just started using that book. So they're probably going to, by the end of the month they'll be getting down to where they'd be using it up. It's a six-across book. Take the last five pages, okay?"

"Okay," the Digger said.

"Don't take no more'n that," the driver said. "You do and they're liable to spot it the next time they use the book." From the floor under the driver's seat he produced a razor knife. "Take them out right along the binder. Don't leave no shreds. Shreds can fall out and get somebody looking. Nice, clean cuts. One page at a time. Don't use where it's perforated. Cut them out right along the binder. Okay?

"Don't take nothing from the other books," the driver said. "The petty-cash box, it's probably got about eighty dollars in it. Leave it be. No stamps, no currency if there's any, no nothing. Five pages of checks and that's all. You give them all to me. I want thirty checks and I don't want no more'n thirty checks taken. Okay?"

"Okay," the Digger said.

"The guy I got," the driver said, "it's going to be important for him the checks went out some time this month, because he's on vacation and he'll be able to prove where he was all the time. We get checks from one of the other books, they start coming in, he's not gonna be protected. Okay?"

"Okay," the Digger said. "How'd you meet him, anyway?"

"It was a business thing," the driver said. "He

5

needed some money and this friend of his sent him around to see me."

"Jesus," the Digger said, "I don't know where the hell you'd be without us guys pressed for dough. You'd probably have to go out and work for a living."

"Some guys," the driver said, starting the Jaguar, "some guys need more'n they have, some guys have more'n they need. It's just a matter of getting us together, Dig, that's all it is."

"I'm thinking of changing sides," the Digger said. "If I get through this without doing time, I'm definitely gonna change sides."

"I recommend it," the driver said, "it's lots more comfortable. Still, it shouldn't take you more'n an hour, and you're fifteen hundred bucks ahead of where you were when you closed up tonight."

"Yeah," the Digger said, "one and a half down, sixteen and a half to go. Someday, my friend, I'm gonna get smart, and when I do, well, I just hope you can find another guy, is all."

"Digger," the driver said as the fat man began to get out, "as long as they keep making women and horses, they'll always be a guy to find. I'll see you in the morning."

2

"You look tired, Dig," Harrington said. "You look like you been up all night or something." Harrington was a foreman at Boston Edison. He worked on Saturdays as a supervisor. He took the Dort Ave bus home every night; he got off a block away from the intersection of Gallivan Boulevard. The Bright Red was on that corner and he stopped in for a couple of cold ones. Week nights he drank his beer and read the *Record*. Saturdays were quiet and he read the *Record* at work, his feet on the desk and a cardboard container of coffee growing cold beside the portable radio. Saturday nights he talked.

"I was," the Digger said. "You'd think a guy as old as I am'd learn sometime, you can't stay up all night 'thout feeling like hell the next day. Not me, I never learn."

"You out drinking or something?" Harrington said.

"Nah," the Digger said, "I was down to the Market, I see this guy. I had something to do. I just didn't get around to going home, is all. I guess I roll in about four. What the fuck, it's Saturday. It's not like it's the middle of the week, you hadda come in here and bust your ass, everybody gets out of work the same time. I can handle it."

"See, I was wondering," Harrington said. "You look like that, I see you looking like that, I was wondering, maybe you got that problem again."

7

"Martinis," the Digger said. "No, I didn't have that. That's a funny thing, you know? I think, I haven't had that kind of problem since the first time I was talking to you. Which was a pretty long time, I think. No, that much I learn, I don't drink no more of that stuff, that fuckin' gin. That stuff'll kill you, I know that much. No, it was something else."

"Broads," Harrington said. "You're a stupid shit, Dig, I always told you that. You're a stupid shit, fool around with the broads. That's dumb. I maybe grew up in Saint Columbkille's, I maybe don't know my ass from third base, I'm out here, the chocolate factory, I still know enough, I don't fool around with no broads. I know that much, at least. You're a dumb shit, staying out all night, fool around with broads. It don't change, Dig, you got to know that. The monkey is the monkey, a cunt is a cunt. Why you wasting your time? Oughta go home and sleep."

"I don't fool around," the Digger said.

"Okay," Harrington said, "you're an asshole. You stayed up till four in the morning because you wanted to. You're a fuckin' asshole. I thought you had more sense. You're too old for staying out like that. No wonder you look like death warmed over. You stayed out because you wanted to. You're an asshole."

"I had a reason," the Digger said.

"Sure you did," Harrington said. "You wanted to get laid, was your reason. You didn't get laid. You're an asshole."

"Look," the Digger said, "I went to Vegas the other week."

"So I hear," Harrington said. "All the high rollers going out to Vegas. 'Look, you dumb shit,' they say to me, 'you can't lose. Up front you pay a grand and they give you eight-twenty back in the chips and the plane ride and the hotel and everything. Broads. You never see the broads like you see the broads in Vegas. Got to fight them off.' So I say, 'Okay. I believe you. How come I gotta tell them the name every bank I ever had an account, huh? It's probably, they want to make sure, I'm a nice fellow, don't want to give the money away, somebody doesn't need it or something. That's probably it.' Oh no, that's not it. It's just to be

8

sure, you know? They don't want no deadbeats. Okay, that's what I'm saying. I'm gonna win, what difference does it make, I'm a deadbeat or not? No difference at all. So all right, I'm not going. They ask me that, the bank accounts, I think they think I'm not gonna win. They think I'm gonna lose, is what they think. Now, they been at it a lot longer'n I have. I think I bet with the smart money this time. I think I'm gonna lose, too, and can't afford to lose. So I'm not going.

"Well," Harrington said, "I dunno if you was around or not, but I take so many kinds of shit I figure, Howard Johnson went into the shit business, twenty-eight flavors. The wife won't let me; I don't have no balls; when am I gonna get smart: all the rest of it. Then everybody goes, and it gets quiet. Beautiful. I actually enjoy coming in here, three or four days, although I think, them millionaires get back from Vegas, I'm gonna have to go down the parish hall, drink tea with the Guild, I expect any peace and quiet.

"Then everybody comes back," Harrington said. "Funny thing, I don't hear nothing. Nothing about broads, I don't see anybody with the big roll, nothing. I start to wonder, what is it? Girls wouldn't do it? Nah, can't be that. All you guys talk nice, use the deodorant there. Steaks tough? Frank Sinatra goes there and the steaks're tough? Can't be that. Everybody got airsick? Nah, all you guy's over the Bulge, some of you were in Korea, every single one of you wins the Medal of Honor, at least in here. Beats me. I just can't understand it. See, I *know* you guys didn't lose no money. You're all too smart for that. You all told me so, a lot. So I finally decide, you're being nice to me. I'm Mickey the Dunce and you're all being nice. Out pricing the Cads with all the dough you won, you're just not telling me because you don't want me to feel bad. You guys, you're saints, you know that, Dig? Saints. I said that to my wife."

"You know," the Digger said, "your principal trouble is, you got a big mouth."

"My wife claims that," Harrington said. "She also says I hang around the wrong type of guys and it

9

gets me in trouble, it won't be her fault. She says a lot of things. But then I say, 'Look, did I go to Vegas and win a million dollars? Not me. I'm too smart for that. Nobody fakes old Harrington into winning no million, no sir.' That shuts her up."

"She think I'm one of the bad guys?" the Digger said.

"She does," Harrington said. "She has said that. But she don't say it no more. I said, 'Look, you like the stereo all right. You give me a lot of stuff and all, but the Digger gets that Stromberg for a hundred and Lechmere's knocking them down for three-fifty, I don't hear no complaints from you.' See, I stand up for you, Digger."

"You interested in a portable radio?" the Digger said.

"No," Harrington said.

"How about a nice color tee-vee?" the Digger said. "RCA, Accucolor, the whole bit."

"No," Harrington said. "I touch the stereo the other night by mistake and I burned myself. I'm gonna be sitting there some fine night, watching the ball game, and some cop's gonna come in. Besides, I can't buy nothing right now, I don't care if you're giving it away. The wife wants a boat. I'm supposed to be saving up for a boat."

"Look," the Digger said, "I need some dough."

"Jesus," Harrington said, "I could use some dough myself. You get ahold the guy that's passing out the dough, give him my name. I could use about thirty-five big ones, right this minute. I got to buy a boat. Get that? I had a boat. I had four rooms over to Saint Columbkille's, I had a nice boat. She don't like that. We got to have a house. 'I can't afford no house,' I said, 'I haven't got the down payment, for God's sake.' She says, 'Sell the boat.' I didn't want to sell my boat. I didn't want to buy the house. I sell the boat. I buy the house. Nine years we had the house, eight of them she's been complaining, we should get another boat. I give up."

"I'm serious," the Digger said.

"You're serious, is it?" Harrington said. "You think I'm just horsing around?"

"You're not serious the way I'm serious," the Digger said. "I need eighteen thousand dollars and I need it right away. Yesterday would've been good."

"Oh oh," Harrington said, "you guys did take a bath out there, didn't you."

The Digger nodded. "The rest of the guys, not as bad as me. But I went in right over my head."

"Jesus," Harrington said, "that why you're out all night?"

"Yup," the Digger said, "I take all kinds of chances and you know what? I'm not even close to even." From the end of the bar a customer demanded service. "Shut your fuckin' mouth, I give you a bat in the head," the Digger shouted. "I'll get to you when I'm damned good and fuckin' ready. Right now I'm talking to a guy." The customer said he thought he could get a drink in the place. "You can get a drink when I feel like gettin' you a fuckin' drink," the Digger said. "Right now I don't feel like it. Paul, 'stead of sittin' down there like a damned dog, come around and give the loudmouth bastard what he wants. Pour it down his fuckin' pants, all I care." At the end of the bar a small man with grey hair got off his stool and came around to the spigots. He started to draw beer. "I got to get even," the Digger said to Harrington, "I got to find a way to get even and that's all there is to it."

"You're not gonna do it pushing radios," Harrington said. "You're not gonna do it that way, I can tell you right now. You, I think you're gonna have to find something a lot bigger'n radios to sell, you expect to make that kind of dough."

"Well, okay," the Digger said, "that's what I was thinking."

"Sure," Harrington said, "you're gonna have to sell the place, here."

"No," the Digger said.

"Whaddaya mean, 'No'?" Harrington said. "You haven't got anything else you can sell. You don't dress that good, you can't sell suits. You got a car there, isn't bad, but you got to get around and you couldn't get more'n a grand for it if you sold it anyway. What the hell else can you do, sell your house? Can't do

11

that. Some guy make you a price on the wife and kids?"

"Well," the Digger said, "I mean, there's other ways of raising money."

"Not without taking chances," Harrington said. "That kind of money, you either got in the bank and you go in and you take it out, or else you got it in something else and you go the bank and you practically hand it over to them, or else you go the bank with a gun and you say, 'Gimme everybody else's money.' There's no other way, and that last one, that's risky."

"There's other ways," the Digger said. "Look, this place. You know what I hadda do, get this place? I hadda get up off the floor, is what I hadda do. Johnny Malloy, I get out of the slammer and Johnny Malloy gives me a job and no shit. Me, I figured, it's temporary, I got to have something to do. I never had any idea of running a barroom all my life."

"What's the matter with running a bar?" Harrington said. "Nothing the matter with that. I wished I had a good bar to run."

"Sure," the Digger said, "but that's it. Takes money, get a bar. I didn't have money. All I had was a goddamned record. Was all I could do, keep the Probation looking the other way while I was working here. So, Malloy gets the cancer. He knew he had it. He says, there wasn't anybody else had the money, wanted to buy it. They're all laying off. He told me that. 'Wait it out and steal it off the wife, they got in mind. Bastards. I'll sell it to you for what it's worth. Not what I could get for it if I was all right and I just wanted to sell. What it's worth. That's about twice what I am getting offers for.'

"I said, 'John, I haven't got what the place's worth. You know that,'" the Digger said. "'I'm working for you, for Christ sake. I shouldn't even be doing that. You're taking a chance with the license, I'm taking a chance with the Probation, what the hell. I can't buy this place.'

"He says, 'You quit too fast, my friend. What I got in mind, you just keep on working for me, only I won't be here. You work for the wife. Only instead of me keeping what I got left after I pay for the stock and the lights and you and all, you pay for the stock and that, and pay her like she was working for you, and you keep what's left. You do that long enough, she's all right, the kids finish school, I don't have to worry about none of that stuff because I trust you, and you end up with the place. Me, what the hell I want with money? Where I'm going, money's no good. What I need is, somebody who's gonna pay money to Evelyn.'

"I said, 'John, okay, all right, sure. But the license. I can't get on no license. You want your wife onna license?' He says, no, he don't want that. Somebody'd take it away from her. He says, 'Look, whyn't you see what your brother can do, the Governor. Try for a pardon.'

"So I do it," the Digger said. "I go see my holy brother and I ask him, does he know anybody. See, by then he's almost getting over it, I did time. Well, no, he don't *know* anybody, but then he's in pretty thick with Bishop Hurley there. Maybe Hurley knows somebody. So it's this way and that, and then I get this call from this rep I never heard of before, will I meet him? Sure I'll meet him. So I meet him, and he's got quite a lot to say, how do I like the weather and what about the way the Red Sox're doing, all kinds of shit, and finally he gets to the point: he wants five hundred bucks. For what he don't say, why he wants it from me, but he knows me and he knows I want this pardon, which I didn't tell him, and he says, 'Running for office, it's very expensive. I got this printing bill.' Then he shows me this bill, it's all beat to shit. He's been carrying it around for probably two years, ever since he got elected, showing it to six or eight guys a week. That's how I could do it, boy, get even: all I need's one of them printing bills. Anyway, it's for five hundred and thirty bucks and he says, 'I dunno how I'm gonna pay it.'

"I come back to Malloy," the Digger said. "I ask him and he says, 'Hit him the five. That's cheaper'n I figured.'

"Now I don't know this rep from a hole inna ground," the Digger said, "and reps don't give pardons, governors do that. But I do it. Two months later, the pardon comes through. And it's a good thing, too, because Malloy's got trouble hanging on. 'Now we got to get an appraiser,' he says. I say, 'What the hell we need an appraiser for? Tell me what it's worth. I'll pay it.' He says: *We* don't need an appraiser, you need an appraiser. You want to get on the license, don't you?' Okay. He tells me, fifty-four K. Now the appraiser comes in. He looks around. 'Fifty-four thousand,' he says. He was here probably twenty minutes. Two grand he charges. I thought that was kind of high. I said, 'You work pretty fast.' He says, old hundred-a-minute, 'I'm an expert appraiser. Been at it a long time, particularly bars and restaurants. Experience, that's what does it.' He leaves and Malloy says, 'Another thing that does it: his brother-in-law's on the Licensing. Now you're gonna get on the license.'

"Now that's the way it is," the Digger said. "I learn fast. I been in the can, it's all right, I still got room for more things I can learn. 'You see?' Malloy says. 'You're gonna do all right now. You're okay to be on the license, and now you're gonna get the license. Take care Evvie.'

"I think Malloy was probably dead about a month," the Digger said. "He didn't last long after he got things taken care of the way he wanted. I go see my fat fuckin' brother. Just by way of no harm he says. 'You might've thanked me, getting the pardon and all, you're doing so well now.' I said, 'Thanks? What the hell for? All you did was send the thief around. I paid the five.' He says, 'What five?' I tell him. Turns out he paid a guy a grand. So I ask him, is it the rep? See, the same thing, I'm willing to go the five, he still shouldn't beat the brother out of the grand. No indeed, he says, no such thing. It's another guy. That's funny, I think, and I tell him about the rep, and he says, 'Well, I think probably I'm gonna check that out.' And he does.

"Now I get another telephone call," the Digger said. "The rep again. Will I meet him. I meet him. I meet him inna Parker House. He says, 'I certainly want to thank you, the loan you give me, and now I want to pay you back.' Hands me this envelope. Five-thirty in it. I count it and I say, 'Here's thirty back. I loaned you the five.' He gets this dumb expression on his face. 'Oh yeah,' he says, 'now I remember you, you cheap fuck.' "

"You should've called a cop," Harrington said.

"I could've," the Digger said. "I could also've called the ghinny Pope in his fuckin' bubbletop limousine, I could've done that, too. Would've done me about as much good.

"Now you look at that," the Digger said. "The rep, the guy with the brother-in-law, my fine fat brother. What does he produce? Every single month for fourteen years I been sending Evvie Malloy three hundred. Gimme about six more years, I own this place, the way the deal finally worked out. 'The place took care of O'Dell,' Malloy said to me, 'it took care of me and it'll take care of Evvie and take care of you. Take care the place, Digger.' He was right. I took care the place. I worked like a bastard. I produced. My brother, he's just as big as me, he's got to eat a lot, you got to eat a lot, you weigh two-ninety, what's he done? I eat at home, what the wife cooks. He's throwing down the lobsters at the Red Coach. He's got a nice Electra Two and a Q. I got to hump it around, find something used that I can afford. After I find it, I get hell for buying it. He's got the place down to Onset, his cottage, it's got eight or nine rooms, a couple baths up and one down, it's a cottage. I got three boys and a girl and I practically got to hock the Social Security to get half a bath in the, where the pantry was, I got a house. He's got a two-car garage, I got no garage at all, in the summer I get the same view of Morgan's lawn, which he never cuts, I had in the winter. The snow and all, it looks better in the winter. In the winter my fuckin' brother's down to Delray for a couple weeks, I see where he goes to Ireland in the fall. Now what I want to know is this, how come them guys? How come them guys and not me."

Harrington drank some beer. "You're pulling your joint," he said. "God's punishing you. Pretty soon you're gonna get hair on your hands and moles on

15

your face and pimples on your ass. Everybody'll be able to tell. Don't do your brains any good, either. Keep it up, you're gonna turn simple, and you don't have far to go, either, you was to ask me. Three Our Fathers and fifty Hail Marys and a good Act of Contrition. Our Blessed Mother don't go for your filthy habits, you know."

"Fuck you," the Digger said. "I listened to you plenty of times. All I was doing was thinking out loud."

"You listened to me," Harrington said, "I was buying the beer. That's the rule: guy that buys the beer does the talking. Now you know what I'm gonna do? I'm gonna go home. You're thinking, the kind of thinking you do, I don't want to be around when you do it."

3

AT ELEVEN THIRTY the Digger closed up. The small man with grey hair took a long time locating his jacket and lunchbox. "For the love of Mike, will you come on?" the Digger said.

"Some son of a bitch stole my paper," the small man said. "I didn't even finish reading it. I think I had about half a beer since I get in here this after, and now some son of a bitch steals the paper."

"Paul," the Digger said, holding the door, "I'm not paying you. Got that? No money. Thanks for your help, but no dough."

"I was on my feet about six hours," the small man said.

"You were on the tap for six hours too," the Digger said. "I loan you money and you don't pay me back. You're into me for thirty or forty bucks and I never asked you for it and you never paid me back. You come home from the track and you're tapped out and I stand you a couple beers and I listen to you, what horrible luck you got, and then I give you five, you don't have to ask the old lady for carfare, she's gonna know you lose. And you always take it. Now the thing for you to do is, shut the fuck up and go home."

The Digger drove to Copley Square and parked his car in front of the Public Library. A sleepy drunk sat up on the steps, then stood and walked unsteadily toward the car. He removed a dirty cloth from his left hip pocket. The Digger locked the driver's side door. The drunk was very old. He stopped and swayed and said: "Polish your car and watch it for you, mister?"

The Digger straightened up. "No," he said. The drunk swayed. "And if I come back here and I see a lot of scratches on the fuckin' thing I'll come find you and take you apart, you fuckin' old wino, you understand that?"

The drunk, swaying, replaced the rag in his pocket. He turned slowly and went back up the steps.

The Digger entered the Boylston garage on the Huntington side and took the elevator to the third tier. At Row D he found a mustard-colored Coupe de Ville with a gold vinyl roof. It had Maryland plates.

The Digger tried his square-butted key in the driver's side door. It worked. It also worked in the ignition. He drove the Cadillac down the ramps to the exit. There was a sleepy kid in a blue Eisenhower jacket on duty.

"I lost my check," the Digger said. On the attendant's booth there was a sign: "Lost ticket must show license and registration."

"You gotta pay the max," the kid said. "Three-fifty."

"Here," the Digger said. He presented a five-dollar bill. The kid gave him change. "That's a screwing," the Digger said. "I was only in here since six."

"Yeah, yeah," the kid said, "read me the whole act if you want. I could make you get undressed and everything, you know."

"I know," the Digger said.

At Logan International Airport the Digger took the "Arrivals" lane and put the Cadillac into an empty space in front of the ground-level entrance to United Airlines. He got out of the car and locked it. At the top of the electric stairs he turned left and walked toward the bar. He found a short, swarthy man seated at a table for two at the east windows. He sat down. He put the key in front of the man.

"Where is it?" the man said.

18

"Right down to the meter," the Digger said. "Right down in front."

"You were supposed to put it inna regular garage," the man said.

"He didn't tell me that," the Digger said. "He said, 'Leave it in front of the United terminal˙ and take the keys in.' That's what I did."

"There's liable to be some fuckin' State Trooper watchin' it, I go out," the man said.

"That's your problem," the Digger said. "You should take it up with him, is what I think."

"I don't give a fuck what you think," the man said. "Key okay?"

"Yup," the Digger said.

"Okay," the man said, starting to get up.

The Digger grabbed him by the left arm and the man sat down again. "There's another thing he told me, he told me you were gonna have some money belonged to me."

"You get that from him," the man said.

"You can get your arm fixed over to the Mass General," the Digger said. "They're open all night, they never close. Your face, too. The Boston City's open all night, too, they got an emergency room, but guys I seen afterwards, I was to make a choice if I was you I'd go the Mass General. Get up five hundred and save the beef on the Blue Cross, is my advice."

"Two hundred," the man said.

"Five hundred," the Digger said. "This was hurry-up, and it's not my usual line of work. I did it, I said I'd do it, the five. Gimme the five, I break your fuckin' nose so you know I mean business."

"You got to leave go my arm," the man said.

"I'll leave go," the Digger said. "You keep it in mind, I can move fast enough I caught you the first time. Nothing funny, the next time I get you, you're gonna need treatment." The Digger let go.

The man reached into his left-hand pants pocket and removed a few bills. He put them on the table and started to get up.

"Siddown," the Digger said.

The man sat down. The Digger counted the bills. "Okay," he said, "you can go."

19

"Thanks a whole fuckin' bunch," the man said.

"Don't give me no shit," the Digger said. "I know who you are. I know what your fuckin' name is and I know what you fuckin' do. I got a dime or so and you tried to screw me. I decided I want to drop one of them dimes, call somebody I know in Boston P.D., you're gonna need more'n one Cadillac to save your greasy ass."

"Fuck you," the man said. He started to get up again, warily.

"It's okay," the Digger said. "I'm satisfied. You can go now. Cheap ghinny pisspot."

"I could kill you, you know," the man said.

"I don't know any such fuckin' thing," the Digger said. "You never made a pass at me, well, you better make a good one, is all. You'd be lying inna window down to Tessie's before the sun came up, and I'd be having a beer on your luck. Fuck off."

The short, swarthy man left. The Digger beckoned a pock-faced waitress. "Wild Turkey," he said. "Double."

"It's almost closing," she said.

"Two Wild Turkeys," the Digger said. "I gotta ride the trolley, I might as well start off first class."

In the floodlights on the apron of the terminal to the north, two priests escorted a large number of middleaged people toward a Northeast 727. Each of them carried a TAP flight bag, white and green.

The waitress came back. She put the drinks on the table. "Three-fifty," she said.

The Digger put a five on the table. "Keep it," he said. "What's that?"

"Pilgrimage, most likely," she said, squinting. "Those're Portuguese Airlines bags. They connect with TAP in New York. Probably going to Fatima."

The Digger watched the passengers straggle aboard after the waitress had left. He finished the first Wild Turkey and raised the second to his lips. "Jesus Christ," he said to himself, 'I think I'd rather take the trolley."

4

"IS THAT FUCKIN' PAPER here yet?" The Greek began talking as soon as he had shut the door of the sparsely furnished office of The Regent Sportsmen's Club, Inc., at 236 Beacon Street, Boston. His black hair was shiny from recent washing; more black hair bloomed from the collar of his white polo shirt.

"Greek," said Croce Torre, also known as Richie Torrey, "I meant to tell you before, what a great thing you are to start off a week." Torrey had a belly. He was grinning.

"Look," the Greek said, "the start of the week's most of the week, in my end of things. I got today and I got tomorrow to get this new stuff squared away so I can take care my regular business. A week and a half's already lost. The longer I wait, the more shit I get, I finally go around. I mean, I can't hack around the rest of my life with this goddamned thing, you know? We're gonna do it, for Christ sake let's do it."

On the other side of the office, Miller Schabb sat at a grey metal desk and muttered into the telephone. "Yeah, Herbie, yeah, I hear you. I know, it's . . . Yeah, the busy season. Well, there's another season too, Herbie, isn't there, not quite so busy. You told me about that one yourself. Nobody in the world wants airplanes then. You get my point? I'm still going to be wanting airplanes. That's if I get my air-plaines now. You can't give me airplanes now, when I want them, you're not going to see much of me later on, you follow me?"

"Look," Torrey said, "I don't run the U.S. Mail, you know? The stuff just got here. It come in, it was here the first thing. Must've, maybe it come in Saturday."

"Well," the Greek said, *"okay.* Let's have it so we can see what we got to work with here." He removed his blue and white cord sports jacket. His biceps stretched the woven fabric of the polo shirt into a coarse mesh.

"How old're you, Greek?" Torrey said.

"Forty-one," the Greek said. "Gimme the fuckin' paper, will you?"

"Miller's got the paper," Torrey said. "He wanted to look it over. He'll be off in a minute, so calm down for Christ sake. You lived forty-one years, you look great, you can afford a couple minutes. Sit down and relax. Christ, I wished to God, I'm thirty-one and I wished to God I looked as good as you do."

The Greek rubbed his middle. It was flat. "You don't look like I do because you don't work at it like I do."

Schabb said, "That's right, Herbie. Now you're getting the idea: when you got airplanes up the gazoo, I'm going to be a nice fellow to know. No, Herbie, no, I wouldn't threaten you."

"The first thing I do, every morning," the Greek said, "over to the Y. I'm there when they open, seven o'clock. I play handball an hour. Swim half a mile. Forty laps. I take a little steam, then shower and I shave. I get dressed, I go over the diner in the Square, bowl of Total and black coffee. Good solid meal and it don't put any fat on you, something happens and you haven't got time for lunch, you're still all right. Three years I've been doing that. See, you get older, you got to do something. I didn't use to have to do anything at all, keep in shape. Now I do."

"I couldn't take that," Torrey said. "You probably have to get up about six to do that."

"Six thirty or so," the Greek said.

"Yeah," Torrey said, "well, see, I couldn't've done

that today. Last night, Sunday night, okay? Nice quiet night. I was married, I didn't use to do anything Sunday night. Watch the tube or something. But last night, I'm down to Thomasina's there. White clam sauce. Few drinks, couple bottles of wine. Then we go up the Holiday, very good group up there. Pick up this girl, we go back to my place, she's got to make an omelette, okay? By now, two in the morning. Cheese omelette, little more white wine, time we finish eating the omelette, it's after three thirty."

"Then you ate her," the Greek said. "Then it's almost four thirty. No, you're right. You couldn't've got up with me."

"There ain't no calories in muffin," Torrey said. "I don't say I did it, you know, but if I did, that won't put any weight on you."

Schabb said, "No, Herbie, no Electra. You put an Electra out there on the end of the ramp, half my trip's going to see it and blow right away. 'Oh no, Mill, not that coffee grinder. Them things come down.' They got a reputation. . . . I don't care what they did to them, they still got a reputation. You got to give me a jet, Herbie."

"Just kind of a degenerate, is all," the Greek said. "You're a fuckin' degenerate, Richie. I dunno how you can look in the fuckin' mirror in the morning."

"My friend," Torrey said, "it was a good enough night, I can't. I can't even *see* the mirror. Last Wednesday, there, I go to the ballgame. Then afterwards we go to this club, all the college kids and secretaries go."

"Whyn't you hang around playgrounds or something?" the Greek said. "Leave the kids alone, you fuckin' degenerate, you're giving them bad habits."

Schabb raised his voice: "Now *look,* Herbie. You can think anything you want. The fact is, I bought three planes from you. I filled the one I had and the other two're going to be filled and if I don't fill the other two, I'm still good for the money and you know it. You try to get that from the Knights of Columbus before they take off. You just try it."

"Yeah," Torrey said, "well, I can see you don't know much about kids any more, Greek. I pick up

23

this kid and we go back and you know what it was? Strawberry."

"You're shitting me," the Greek said.

"I am not shitting you," Torrey said. "Strawberry. They got that spray now. Now, you old fart, you tell me I'm teaching bad habits a kid's got strawberry in the beaver before I ever meet her. You just tell me that."

"I don't fuckin' believe it," the Greek said. "She must've been a hooker or something."

"She's a file clerk down to this insurance company," Torrey said. "She's no hooker, because I didn't give her no money. Hell, you look at her you figure, she walked in a bar by mistake, thought it was a church. You'd just be wrong, that's all. She likes getting it, nothing more'n that. How about that, Greek, huh?"

"You guys're gonna take over the world," the Greek said. "The next thing, guy wants to get blown, he's gonna have to taste like London Broil."

"Sure," Torrey said, "she's having dinner, you're having dessert. Thats a great idea, Greek."

"Yeah," the Greek said, "well, I tell you, I think I'm gonna get myself a nice place way the hell out in the country and go out there with the family and start a chicken farm. I'm not gonna bring kids up in a world, people walking around with vanilla pussy, hot fudge cocks. This fuckin' country's going to the dogs, you know that, Richie? Guys like you."

Schabb said, "That's a hell of a lot better, Herbie. Yeah. Yeah. Seven-twenty-seven's fine, Herbie. Now, read it back to me."

"You oughta try it before you knock it, Greek," Torrey said. "You look good enough. You could still make out."

"I look good because I want to look good and I work at it," the Greek said. "Not because I want to go around like a goddamned pervert. You want to go around in them yellow things, shirts, pants, the white shoes, it's probably all right, you look like a nigger pimp. Don't matter to you. I got some self-respect."

"You're afraid," Torrey said. "You work so hard taking showers there, you probably don't think, you're not sure you can get it up."

"Also," the Greek said, "also, I need to look good.

24

Your action, you can wear a fuckin' *dress* if you want. People're probably gonna laugh at you some, but that's all right. You take me, your average stiff borrows some, he thinks I collect my own, he doesn't pay. So, he maybe starts thinking about not paying, he kind of looks at me out there, he thinks, 'Son of a bitch can do the work himself, I don't pay.' So he pays. I'm up the hundred two hard guys cost me. Plus which, I don't get the kind of heat you get when you start moving guys around personal. Nice and peaceful is the way I like things."

Schabb said, "All right. That's fine, Herbie, you got a deal. Always a pleasure to talk to you." He hung up. He smiled. "I got the plane for Columbus Day," he said to Torrey. To the Greek he said, "Good morning, Greek."

"You know you got a degenerate for a partner?" the Greek said. "He's eating little kids."

"You eating kids, Richie?" Schabb said. "You ought to be ashamed of yourself."

"I can't help it," Torrey said. "You remember the other night, there. Everything goes black and then I did it again."

"Told you about the strawberry one, I guess," Schabb said. "Unbelievable huh?"

"I don't believe it," the Greek said. "I should've gone in the Church like my mother was always after me to do. I can't take this kind of thing. You got some paper for me to see, Mill?"

"Yeah," Schabb said, "right here." He removed a thick packet of papers, check-sized, held together with a rubber band, from the desk. He tossed it across the room to the Greek; it landed on the second grey metal desk. The Greek moved behind the desk and slipped the packet out of the band.

"You had some trouble," Torrey said to Schabb.

"Yeah," Schabb said. "You'd think we're trying to steal airplanes, 'stead of buying them, probably the best customer he's got. One more like this and we'll have to hijack the damned things. For a guy that's always griping about how lousy business is, he's sure awful tough to do business with."

"You count this stuff?" the Greek said. He was sorting the papers into three piles."

"I looked at it, is all," Schabb said. "There's quite a bit of money there. Maybe the boys didn't win the whole State after all."

"I make it one-eighty-eight K," the Greek said.

"That's quite a bit of money," Torrey said.

"What'd the plane cost us?" the Greek said.

"Twenty-eight," Schabb said.

"Hotel," the Greek said.

"Three K, promo, free drinks and that stuff, tips for the bells," Schabb said.

"Pretty high, you ask me," the Greek said. "We deliver the fish, we also got to pay to ice them down. How many guys we had?"

"Eighty," Schabb said.

"Eighty K in front from them," the Greek said, "sixty-six K, was it, we hand back in counters?" Schabb nodded. "What'd that cost us?"

"Twenty-two," Schabb said.

"Twenty-five K, counters and promo, twenty-eight for the plane," the Greek said, "any other expenses?"

"You wanna count the rent and phone here?" Torrey said. "It's pretty steep, three bills, lights're extra, they do give you the air conditioning."

"Damned nice of them," the Greek said. "No. Fifty-three, expenses. One-thirty-five starting out with the paper, we collect it all."

"Not bad at all," Schabb said.

"We collect it all?" Torrey said. "What is this shit, we collect it all."

"Just what I said," the Greek said, "We collect it all, we got one-thirty-five here. We don't collect it all, we got less. Plus the points, of course."

"Greek," Torrey said, "I don't understand this. That's what we got you for, you know, collect it all."

"I could use a coffee," the Greek said.

"Mill," Torrey said, "get coffee."

"Why should I get coffee?" Schabb said. "I don't even want coffee. I told you anyway, we ought to get a pot and put it in here."

"That don't work," Torrey said. "I had one up to the place in Lynn there, somebody was always going home at night and leaving the thing plugged in. So, you get one of two things. You got a pot that's practically welded itself together, all the coffee stewed away, and that's useless. Or else, there's enough coffee, you come in the next day and you got a pot you're never gonna get rid of the taste of it. And somebody's always spilling it. It's easier."

"For a muffin man," the Greek said, "you're awful dainty, Richie. I never knew you're so neat."

"Never mind neat," Torrey said. "Mill, willya get coffee for Christ sake?"

"No," Schabb said. "I'm no errand boy. Call somebody up, you want coffee, have them bring it up. You're gonna do that, I'll have a cup myself, matter of fact. Large regular, and a Danish."

"No calls," Torrey said, "I'm expecting a call. I don't want the line tied up."

"Richie," the Greek said, "this is just a waste of time, all right?"

"Looks like it," Torrey said.

"*Mister* Schabb," the Greek said, "me and Richie want coffee. Richie and me, we're not *going* for coffee. *You're* going for coffee, got that? Now, go for coffee. Get me two blacks. Get him what he wants. Pay for it yourself. Don't talk about it no more. Just do it, all right?"

Schabb looked at Richie.

"Don't look at me, Mill," Torrey said. "The man tried to tell you nice, I tried to tell you nice, you don't want to be told that way. Now you got told the other way. Get the fuck out of here and get the fuckin' coffee and just do it, all right?"

"I guess I am the errand boy," Schabb said, getting up.

"No," the Greek said, "you're just the guy that's nice enough to go out and get coffee for everybody and so me and Richie here can have a little discussion, just between him and me. You had a little more experience, none of this would've happened."

After the door closed, the Greek said, "Is he all right?"

"He's a great guy," Torrey said. "The thing about him, he's perfect, you know? Because he still, basi-

27

cally he's still a businessman, you know what I mean? He still thinks like they do. He likes the pussy probably a little more'n the average married guy oughta, and he's kind of a wise-ass, but he still, he's still a businessman. He tried to line up the bar association."

"Hey," the Greek said, "that'd be something."

"Wouldn't it, though?" Torrey said. "All them bastards with a license to steal, getting screwed themselves for a change."

"Wouldn't be bad for dough, either," the Greek said. "Some of those guys, you can really make out on them. They got good dough. The flashy ones in the knit suits and El Ds. Take them right over the fuckin' hurdles. They think they know fuckin' everything."

"He'd do it for nothing," Torrey said. "Miller hates lawyers. He thinks he should've beat that fraud thing."

"Well, shit," the Greek said. "I thought he got an S.S. out of it."

"Sure," Torrey said. "Myself, I think he made out beautiful. A suspended and a fine and he hadda make restitution. So, a thousand the fine, thirty thou I think it was, they got him for, he told me himself, well, he didn't actually tell me but I could tell, you know? He got close to seventy-five before they nailed him. So, forty K profit, he don't go the can, he's still mad as hell. 'I had the fix in,' he says. 'It was in the bag. I give, my lawyer tells me it's five for him and ten for the prosecutor and something for the judge, it's gonna be dismissed. No evidence or something. So, I pay it over. Then, whammo, I get it right between the eyes. I got screwed.' "

"So," the Greek said, "big deal. He got fucked. I can understand that. But still, he comes out of it all right. I clouted a car when I was a kid and I done three months up the Lyman School. The guy got the car back, too. I would've taken his deal. I wouldn't care if somebody did blow smoke up my ass."

"That's what I tell him," Torrey said. "That's what I'm saying, he thinks like a businessman. He don't know, is all. All he knows is he can't get bonded no

28

more and he don't trust anybody that looks straight. I tell you, Greek, we got ourselves a fine fat gaffer in this guy."

"It's all right to talk about things in front of him then," the Greek said.

"He is joined up," Torrey said. "I personally guarantee it. He is *in*."

"See," the Greek said, "I was nineteen, I get out of the training school there, I make myself a little promise. I was, I wasn't going back. Well, I didn't. And one way I didn't, I watch what I say in front of guys. You're sure."

"You can talk in front of him," Torrey said.

"He knows what we got to do, then," the Greek said.

"He knows about the man," Torrey said. "He knows the guy in Worcester and he knows, he knows about, the guy in, how we got to send down to Providence. I put it right on him, he was telling me how we could take that chickenshit thing I had going up there in Lynn and turn it into something. I said, 'Look, I'm interested, no question. But there's maybe some things you don't understand about this kind of operation, the way it works, what you got to do, you know?'

"He says, 'Look, I can guess. I been around some. You don't need to draw me a picture.' And I say, 'Mill, I'm *gonna* draw you a picture. There's one thing I learn, a thing like this, everybody that's in it better know exactly what he's in. See, I don't want you go running to the man or something, telling me you didn't know what you're getting yourself into. So I'm telling you right now, your own personal information and nobody else's, because if I catch you telling anybody else, I'm gonna kill you, all right? A piece of this, we got to work this on the okay from Worcester, and we get that okay, there's a price on it. We got to pay the money down to Providence there, all right? You understand that?'

"He says, 'Yeah.' I say, 'You mean it now. You're getting in this, you're gonna be connected, is all there is to it. Because you can't *do* this, you're not connected. You understand that.'

29

"He says, 'I understand.' He says, 'You're not tell-ing me anything I didn't know, I started talking to you. I was looking for you, for Christ sake. You think I went looking for somebody, I didn't know the guy I was looking for?'

"I say, 'Okay, then, you're in. But you know, it's like getting married, it's like getting married in *Italy,* there, you know? We never had no divorce, we haven't got any now. You're in, you're in, and you stay in. That means you go out someday and you take your medicine, you go inna grand jury or something, okay, that's what you do. You go out and you take your fuckin' medicine. You don't, I come around and wreck you personally, because I have to. Okay?'

"He says," Torrey said, "he says, 'Okay. I told you, I don't have no objections.'

"I say, 'I hope so. I hope you got it clear in your mind. I'm responsible for you, you come in. I got to be sure and you got to be sure, because I got to cover my ass. I been covering my ass for a long time. I know how to do it. I know, I bring a guy in, I'm taking a chance, is what 'm doing. I don't take no big chances. I wanted big chances, I'd take my own goddamned tours. I don't. So, you get *him* in the shit, I'm the guy gonna have to do down there, explain how come, and that I can't do. So I better not have to, Mill. There's a lot of guys'd like to have another crack at the man, they're not satisfied, he's already doing time, they figure, they figure he's gonna get out someday. That they don't want. They're looking for guys like you that didn't always understand everything they said they understood. You better not be ·one of them. Because, you turn out to be one of them, I'll have to do something. And I'll do it, Mill, no matter how much I like you personally. I'll do it.' He says, 'Okay,' He's okay, Greek. Now what is this shit, if we collect?'"

"Well," the Greek said, "I look at this stuff, all right? Three kinds of paper." He tapped the stack nearest his right hand with his right forefinger. "Jew-ish paper. Names I recognize. Easy stuff. Big sports with the fat-ass yachts and the golf carts in Newton. Every one of them drives the Cad. Used to playing, used to losing, used to paying. No pissing and moaning at all. I floated some of them a fast hundred K for a land deal now and then, it's a Sunday and they're inna hurry and the banks're closed. Only thing is, they're so used to losing, they don't lose all that much. I figure there's less'n half what we got here, there. What we oughta get off them guys, we oughta get a piece of what they pay the cunts to fuck them. Then we'd really make out."

The Greek tapped the middle stack. "Not one goddamned name in here I recognize. The addresses I do. Needham, Wellesley, Beverly, that kind of thing. Duxbury, Hingham, Sharon.

"Now I make a guess on that," the Greek said, "professional guys. Doctors, lawyers, guys that fix people's teeth and feet and that kind of stuff. Sweat their balls off twenty years and all of a sudden they're making thirty and they go right out of their fuckin' minds. Get their hair styled, all of a sudden they know everything. First thing they do, they go to Vegas and lose about six K apiece."

"They're guys Mill knew," Torrey said. "I dunno much about them."

"Just what I thought," the Greek said, "I left that out. First thing they do, they get themselves a smartass broker like him, and they lose about two K. That makes them feel so good, they go to Vegas and drop six."

"They got it, though," Torrey said.

"Most of them, yeah," the Greek said. "They just don't know they got it, it's in appreciation onna house or it's in what they can borrow from the bank. They got it, they just don't know they got it. So first you gotta convince them of that, they got it. Then, the next thing, you got to convince them they owe it. See, they're used to getting things, they spend money, they get a new car or they get a boat or a trip or something. Furniture. They already had what they got for this. You got to convince them of that, too. Then, they're not used to a guy like me. They all, they all borrowed money. When they hadda pay the money, guy sends them a letter. They haven't got the money, guy sends them a piece of paper. Any banker inna world's gonna trust a guy, kind of job they got. So I

31

gotta teach them that: I don't trust them. Few calls do it. I snarl at them. They pay. They read all them books. I'll get that."

"So where's the problem?" Torrey said.

"Problem's this," the Greek said, tapping the pile on the left. "These guys I know. Digger Doherty's group, the guys hang around the Bright Red, there. I would have to say, I would have to say if somebody was to ask me, we got twenty-eight K in the Digger and them, and that's gonna be hard to get out. I don't think bringing in them jamokes was such a hot idea."

"We hadda fill the plane," Torrey said. "We had fourteen beds at the hotel, we're gonna have to pay for, at least one night, we don't use them, the whole three nights, they don't rent them to somebody else. Miller told me he was coming up empty, his other prospects. I said I'd see what I could do. So I tried the Digger."

"Richie," the Greek said, "you hang around the wrong type of guys. You know them guys?"

"Yeah," Torrey said, "I know them guys."

"You know them guys," the Greek said, "you don't know them too good. Those're hard Harps. They haven't got twenty-eight K in the one place since the day they're born, all of them put together. In addition to which, they are very tough guys. I used them myself, somebody got it in his head the Greek was running a charity here. I had very good results. The fuckin' Digger, he's got a machinegun. Most guys know the Digger, know he's got a machinegun, it's one of those things everybody knows. There's talk the Digger used the machinegun a couple times. I get the Digger personally, I call in the Digger, I get somebody else he sends around, he's tied up and he can't do that particular one, it don't make no difference. You get the same thing and you get it, too. You get one or two of them bastards from the Bright Red and you send them around to whale the piss out of somebody, they go around and whale the piss out of him. That could give me some trouble. Maybe they decide now, I go to see them, there isn't anybody big enough, come in and whale the piss out of *them*. Then what do I do?"

32

"Two things," Torrey said. "That's only if they welsh. I know the Digger a long time. I know Mikeymike Magro a long time. They're a couple of loudmouth micks, is what they are."

"They can also deliver," the Greek said. "Never mind how much noise they make."

"You gimme a chance to finish," Torrey said, "that's what I'm saying. I know the guy and I don't like the guy, but I got to say, I never see the guy come up short on anything. So, I don't think you're gonna need anybody, go in and whack him. His friends, either. They lose, they pay. I thought of that when I ask them."

"Still, maybe they don't," the Greek said. "Then who's got the problem? You got the problem? No, I got the problem. Which you give me. Which you didn't ask me, was it all right for everything, you're maybe giving me this big fat headache. See, Richie, that's what I don't like, you not asking me, before. I don't want no more of that."

Miller Schabb opened the door after knocking. He carried a large paper bag that was wet at the bottom. "You guys through kissing and hugging?" he said. "Okay for the niggers to come in now?"

"Come on in, Mill," Torrey said. "Shut the fuckin' door and shut your goddamned yap, too, while you're at it. The Greek didn't know where you stood, was all."

Schabb put the bag on a pad of white paper. "Look at that," he said, "goddamned stuff. Gets all over you, got to go out, it isn't even ten o'clock yet and I bet it's ninety already. I tell you something: tonight on the way home, I'm stopping at Lechmere and getting a coffeepot."

"You get it," Torrey said, "you clean it."

"Sure," Schabb said, "sure, I'll clean it. I also sweep out and I clean the toilet, too. That's what I do, Greek, I'm on the shit detail."

"Willya come off it, Mill, for Christ sake?" Torrey said. "Greek don't have nothing against you. He just didn't know. He's getting old, getting worried, he just wanted to be sure."

"Yeah," the Greek said. "See, Mill, somebody

should've told you. You got, see, Richie's the kind of partner you got to watch. He gets himself all pissed off or something and then he goes out and does something, and then everybody else's got to run around and everything trying to cover his ass for him. Richie's okay for a partner if you watch him real close and don't leave him go down the North End and start waving his arms at the cops or something. It don't mean nothing."

"It don't mean nothing," Torrey said, "long as you understand what it means, Greek. This is my business. Miller's in it and you're in it, because I wanted you guys in it. That's all. It's still my business. I can't work it with you guys, either one of you, I'll go get some new guys and run it with them. I can do it. I'm the guy with the okay, don't forget."

Schabb distributed the cups of coffee. "I dunno what I'm gonna forget," he said, "since I wasn't here and all. You guys mind telling me what this is all about?"

"The Greek's afraid he can't do his job, is all," Torrey said. "He don't want to admit it, but that's basically what it is."

"I don't like that kind of talk, Richie," the Greek said. "I come in here, I been doing this more'n twenty years, putting money out and getting it back in again, and I'm as cold as a nun's cunt. You, you had a good idea, now you don't want to listen to anybody else, you want to start something, pretty soon you got the FBI putting three guys in white sedans out there and all. Okay, don't listen. Be a big asshole. Then when you fuck it up good and everybody's good and screwed, you can tell everybody, you screwed it up because you're just like a little kid and you wanted to, I guess." The Greek leaned forward, toward Richie. "Now you can do that, you want," he said, "you can. But I was here when you got here and I'll be here when you're gone, I still got my regular business. And you're not gonna fuck me up with it, clear?"

"What he's afraid of," Torrey said to Schabb, "he's afraid the guys down the Bright Red'll tell him to go home, and make him cry."

"I don't know those guys," Schabb said. "I was after some other guys, I know them from around town. You see them various places. I had about thirty of them, the movers that don't always go home at night, like they're supposed to, I figured them for naturals. Except I didn't figure, I was talking the last two weeks in July, first week in August. That's when these birds take the family to the Cape and pretend they're behaving themselves. I got about four out of the lot and I was counting on twenty. We could've lost some serious money on that. So I asked Richie."

"Richie give you some bad advice, then," the Greek said. "I'll do the best I can with it this time, but I don't want no more of this. Next time, ask me, too, see what I got to say."

"Okay," Torrey said, "ask him, Mill, is it all right, we got the Holy Name?"

The Greek said, "What?"

"Yeah," Schabb said, "Saint Barbara's Holy Name from Willow Hill there. Going to Freeport over Labor Day. Three glorious days and nights of sun, sand, excitement and luxury living in the glamour center of the Caribbean, a welcome Daiquiri in the well-appointed Casino Lounge, a pineapple in every spacious room, a spectacular view of sparkling beaches and azure water from your own private terrace. Plus: a surprise gift for the ladies, an orchid corsage about the size of a quarter that we get for thirty-eight cents apiece. All for the incredibly low price of three hundred and fifty dollars a couple, including round trip by jet and transfers between the airport and the hotel. I cut the parish school in for five hundred to get the pastor to let me in the door, but I did it."

"Per couple," the Greek said. "They're taking their wives."

"Sure," Schabb said. "One or two of them wanted to know if they could bring the kids, but I said I couldn't arrange it."

"Isn't that something?" Torrey said.

"It sure is," the Greek said. "It's a mess of shit, is what it is. Those guys haven't got ten bucks to put on the table. What're you giving them, counters? How much you staking them?"

"Twenty dollars a couple," Schabb said. "I could've

done a little better, it's a cheap plane ride, but I figured the twenty was enough. That'll get them inside at night."

"It'll get them inside the first night," the Greek said. "Daddy'll lose the twenty while the little woman watches. Then he'll lose six bucks more. Then they'll go back the room and eat the fuckin' pineapple. Why the fuck're we giving away pineapples, for Christ sake? Who wants a goddamned pineapple?"

"Everybody wants a pineapple," Schabb said. "They started doing that in Hawaii. Pretty soon the word got around. Now your average clown doesn't think he's been to a resort if there isn't a pineapple on the commode when he walks in the room."

"Yeah," the Greek said. "Well, this group, we probably ought to give one *slice* of pineapple. All night long the old lady'll be at him, dropping all that great American dough, gambling. He wasn't so goddamned stupid they could've stayed home and seen a movie on the six bucks. The next two days they spend getting the sun, on which we don't make no money, the way I get it. We'll be lucky we make expenses.

"We get unlucky," the Greek said, "it'll be worse. The silly bastards won't quit. They'll lose their fuckin' shirts and sign everything you put in front of them, and then I'll have to go out and take a lot of washing machines and secondhand cars to write the stuff off. Why in Christ you want them nickel-stealing hot dogs, for, can you tell me that?"

"We're, they're not signing any papers," Schabb said. "The priest thought of that one right off, and I agreed with him. 'No, Father,' I said, 'nothing like that. No credit gambling. Just what they bring with them. We're not that kind of operation, Father, trying to victimize people. Basically, we're just a travel agency. Labor Day's a slack period in the package-tour business. Just a way to keep the airplanes going and the hotels full. Frankly, we expect to take a loss on this, but the hotels make it up to us.'"

"At least you didn't lie to a priest," the Greek said. "What are we gonna do with this?"

"We're gonna take pictures of them," Torrey said. "That first night, they're blowing the twenty, we're

36

gonna, we got this guy with a camera. He's gonna take about eighty pictures of those jerks. Then he's gonna send them back, and Mill's gonna make up a brochure."

Schabb grinned.

"I don't get it," the Greek said.

"It *makes* the flyer," Schabb said. "I talked to the Philadelphia group the other day; they did that. They got a deadhead bunch and they made about sixty dollars on the deal. But then they put it on the brochure: 'The Holy Sucker's Men's Club, Satisfied Customers At Play In San Juan.' Ten pictures of fat guys and women. You should see the business it gets them. The used-car dealers and the appliance distributors and the Rich Kids A.C., the guys who really want to go and have the money we're interested in, they take the pamphlet home. How does the wife argue with them? You've really got something you can work with, then. A trip like this is just something you get through. Then it pays and it pays and it pays, and it just never stops."

"You see, Greek?" Torrey said. "Now you understand? That all right with you?"

"That's pretty fuckin' good," the Greek said. "I got to admit it. That is all right."

"You never would've thought of that, would you, Greek?" Torrey said.

"No," the Greek said. "Just the same as you didn't think how I was gonna get twenty-eight out of guys down in Dorchester there. Just like Mister Schabb there, got himself all steamed up, he's gonna have some empty seats on the plane and he's gonna lose, maybe fifteen thousand, so him and you get together and now as a result we got a pretty good chance of losing twenty-eight, instead. See, there was something you guys didn't think of in a million years, and another thing you didn't think of was to ask me if maybe I thought of something. I'm different than you, Richie," the Greek said, "I always known, I known ever since I got out, and that was a long time ago, I'm the kind of guy that's got to think about things, you know? Because there's certain things I can do and certain things that if I do them, I'm gonna get inna shit. You, I done all right, see? You, you don't."

5

THE DIGGER GOT UP at eleven and asked his wife for ten dollars.

"How come I got to give you ten dollars out of the house money?" Agatha Doherty said. She was thirty-nine years old. She was five feet, three inches tall and she had a trim figure. She wore a nine-dollar tan dress. "You don't give me enough as it is, and then you're always coming back and dipping into it. I've been saving up to get my hair done. I got to have it frosted again."

"I thought you were gonna quit having that," the Digger said. "You're always telling me, how it hurts. And it costs, what?"

"Thirty dollars," she said. "It does hurt, it hurts a lot. They take a crochet hook and they pull your hair out through this cap that's got holes in it. I do it because I thought you liked it. You told me you liked it, you didn't care about the thirty dollars. Now I suppose you're more interested in what you can do with the thirty dollars'n you care how I look any more."

"Oh boy," the Digger said. He was eating four fried eggs, blood pudding and toast. "It *does* look good. I *don't* care about the thirty. You're a good-looking woman. You take care of yourself. I appreciate it. There's very few women I ever see, raised four kids by themselves and look as good as you do. I said that lots of times."

"It's nice to hear," she said. "I don't know as it's

worth ten dollars to me, but it is nice to hear. You shouldn't eat so much, you know. That stuff's all full of cholesterol. You're going to get yourself a nice heart attack if you don't stop stuffing yourself all the time."

"Look," the Digger said, "I quit smoking, right? You remember that? I got off the butts. Well, that don't do the weight no good, you know? You're so worried, how much I weigh, why the hell is it I couldn't get a minute's peace around this house every time I light up a cigarette?"

"I'm not likely to forget you quit," she said. "It was like living with a regular bear. No, I know that helps. And I thought, Well, let him put the blubber on, he'll take it off later. Only you didn't. You just keep on, getting bigger and bigger. I bet you weigh two hundred and fifty pounds."

"I don't," the Digger said. "You want to think so, okay. But I don't."

"You don't," she said, "it's because you weigh more. You're probably up to two-seventy-five. You damned near crushed me, the last time."

"Hey," the Digger said, "quit that kind of talk. What if the kids hear you?"

"If you got up in the morning," she said, "you know, you'd know where they are. They all went over to the pool. Anyway, Anthony's fourteen."

"So what?" the Digger said.

"I don't think he thinks the stork brings them any more," she said.

"Of course he don't," the Digger said. "He's known different since he was six. I think they give him a copy of *Playboy* when he makes his First Communion there. He's the horniest little bastard I ever seen. That still don't mean, he oughta hear his mother talking like a longshoreman."

"I don't see what difference it makes," she said. "He can hear the bed squeaking, you know. As much as you weigh, the whole house probably moves around. He knows about sex and he knows we do it."

"How," the Digger said, "how do you know?"

"Never mind," she said.

"The sheets, probably," the Digger said. "Good. Better he's having wet dreams'n he's going out knocking up some eighth-grader, I could have that on my mind too."

"Now who's talking like a longshoreman?" she said.

"You told me, the kids're out," the Digger said.

"I don't matter of course," she said. "No reason to watch your language around me."

"Look," the Digger said, "are you having your period or something? I ask you for ten bucks, you give me nothing but grief. You don't want to loan it to me, say so, I'll go cash a check."

Aggie Doherty took her handbag from the cupboard. "I'll loan you ten dollars," she said. "That means I get it back."

"Tonight," the Digger said. "When I close up tonight, I'll take it out of the deposit. You'll have it tomorrow morning."

"How come you didn't take it Saturday?" she said, handing him the money. "You should've taken some money when you closed up Saturday, the way you usually do so I don't know how much money you're spending."

"I did," the Digger said.

"Uh huh," she said, "that's what I figured. Then last night after everybody else went to bed, all of a sudden you went out. Now today you need ten more dollars. Who'd you spend all your money on, Sunday night when it's the only night you can spend home with your family and all of a sudden you've got to go out? What can she do for you that I can't do?"

"Look," the Digger said, "you went to bed, nine thirty. Matthew and Patricia went to bed before you. Paul right afterwards. Tony come in about ten thirty and he went to bed. See, I'm such a good father, I take my family the beach on Sunday, it's my day off. The traffic down and the traffic back, I buy practically every kind of hot dog there is in the world, everybody takes rides at Paragon Park, I even give Tony five, so he can go off and see what's female and breathing he can try to get in trouble. I come home with ten or eleven bucks left out of twenty-five I take Saturday night, everybody craps out on the old man by eleven. So I sit and I think and I watch the news,

40

I'm still wide awake. I'm not used to your kind of hours. It's my one night off, for Christ sake, I'm supposed to spend it looking at the newspaper or something? So I go down the Saratoga, see what's going on."

"That's what I asked you," she said, "who was she?"

"I spent four bucks on some drinks," the Digger said. "I meet Marty Jay down there and we talk and I had the four drinks. A guy I know comes along, he's stiff, my big mouth, I told him, he oughta take a cab home. No dough. So I lend him five. I was there a long time, I didn't leave till after two, me and Marty we each leave the kid a buck, we take up the table all that time. So I got a buck and change on me now. I had four lousy drinks and I lend a guy five and now I been out all night in a whorehouse. You better get some fresh news, sweetheart: you can't make out *no*where on ten bucks any more. All I did was have four drinks."

"Martinis, I suppose," she said. "You drink too much, too. That isn't good for the heart. I could smell it on you when I woke up."

"You oughta get your nose frosted instead of your hair," the Digger said. "I was drinking bourbon."

"It's no better for the heart," she said. "Just for my information, what's this ten for? You got another friend who needs a cab?"

"Gas for the car," the Digger said.

"Haven't you got enough gas to get to work?" she said. "You could go to work and take it out of the till."

"I'm not going to work," the Digger said. "What I mean is, first I gotta see a guy. Then I'm going to work."

"Where's the guy live, you need ten dollars' worth of gas," she said, "New York City?"

"The tank's almost empty," the Digger said. He pushed the plate away. "I'll have some coffee if it won't do my heart any harm."

"It won't help it," she said, pouring the coffee. "Of course I keep forgetting, the way that car uses gas you probably couldn't go more'n twenty miles on a tank anyway."

"You know," the Digger said, "I could get ten dollars easier, I was to go over the Poor Clares and beat them out of it. And they haven't even got ten dollars, to hear them talk, although I see they probably got a hundred thousand dollars' worth of real estate. Jesus Christ, are you gonna start in on the car again?"

The Digger drove a 1968 Olds Ninety-eight convertible. It was dark grey and had a red leather interior. It had factory air conditioning.

"I'm just being practical," she said, "I don't think you need such an expensive car."

"I had that car two years," the Digger said. "For two years you've been being practical about it. Two years and I haven't spent a dime on it except for tires and gas and stuff. Not one dime. I think that's pretty good. That's a good car. It's well built, just like you. No repair bills."

"It's still a great big car," she said. "It burns a lot of gas and you have to buy high-test. I drive it, the one day a year I'm lucky enough to get the car, it's very hard for me to drive. If you'd drive a smaller car, I could have a Volkswagen."

"It is a great big car," the Digger said. "As you just remind me for a couple hours, I'm a great big man. I need a big car. I can't get in one of them puddlejumpers. I get in, I can't move. They're not built for a man my size. I'd break the seat down in a week. Friday night, I was in one of them Jaguars. I couldn't move. I thought to God, I'm going to die before I get out of this thing and they'll have to bury me in it."

"Who do you know, owns a Jaguar?" she said. "You told me you were working Friday night."

"I did and I was," the Digger said. "I went out, after."

"For what?" she said.

"To see a guy," the Digger said. "I went down the Saratoga and this guy I know, he wanted to show me his new car, is all."

"Jerry," she said, "you worry me. The weight's going to kill you. You spend way too much money. You drink too much. You got friends I never see, I

42

don't know their names, this guy with a Jaguar. What'll I do, Jerry, with four kids in school? What'll I do if something happens to you?"

"Ride around in a big car every day and enjoy yourself," the Digger said. "How the hell do I know what you're gonna do, be doing when I'm dead. I'll be dead. Won't be nobody dipping in the house money, at least, which I notice is up around sixty bucks a week. I'm always dipping into my dough for twenty more around Thursday, after I go and give you the forty Monday. And do I give you a load of shit about that? I do not."

"Don't you talk to me about what it costs to run this house," she said. "If I spend forty-five dollars a week on food, most of it goes down your gullet. The kids go off to school on ten cents' worth of Wheaties, wearing cheap shoes I can get for them in the Basement, and if Paul ever sees a pair of pants Tony didn't wear for a year first, he won't know what to do with them."

"Well," the Digger said, "at least he won't have to scrape the come offa them."

"Jerry!" she said.

"Okay," the Digger said, "okay."

"He's your son," she said.

"He's your son too," the Digger said.

"I don't think it's a mother's place to talk to a boy about sex," she said.

"I didn't say it was," the Digger said. "No point in it anyway, it'd be like telling a priest about the Apostle's creed."

"It would be now," she said. "I told you a long time ago, the time'd come to talk to him."

"About six months ago," the Digger said. "He's been coming in fast every night for about a year or so, 'Hi Mum, Hi Dad,' don't stop to talk to you, runs right upstairs just like he did last night, if he comes down he's wearing different pants. Spends about two hours a day in the flush. Why you think he does that, does them things, huh?"

"It's your fault," she said, "if he is, it's your fault. You just remember that."

"Fault?" the Digger said. "What's this, fault? I'll

43

take the credit, that's what you mean, although I got to say, I don't think I deserve it all, you know what I mean. He takes after his mother a little bit too." She did not answer him. She took the plate off the table and got up and went to the sink. "How come you get embarrassed when I say something like that, there isn't anybody else around?" the Digger said.

Her shoulders sagged. For a while she did not answer. Then without facing him she said, "Jerry, I do the best I can, I really do. I hunt around until I can get things on sale. But you come down here, you've got to have the eggs and the blood pudding I have to shop for special at the delicatessen, two-fifty-six a pound and it's really terrible for you, you eat three pounds a week. You've got the French Shriners that you pay the full price for. Off you go whenever you like in your air-conditioned convertible big car. Can you understand, does that maybe make some sense to you? The trouble is that I'd do anything to make you happy. I love you. *And you know it.* That's what the trouble is."

"Lemme try it for the hundredth time," the Digger said. "Let's see if you can get it through your head this time. I bought the used car. The air conditioning was in it. I agree with you, it's silly. You put the top down, what good's the air? You leave the top up all the time, what do you want a convertible for? The guy had the car before me, he didn't. He wanted the air for rainy days and the top for nice days. Okay, he was buying it, he could have it the way he liked. I didn't put it in. You take it the way you find it. I wouldn't've saved no money, I had the air taken out. It would've cost me money. So I leave it in. Although I think now, I knew how much music it was gonna cost me, I wouldn've paid the extra dough to take it out.

"The shoes," he said. "It's the same with everything I wear. I got trouble getting fitted. I don't go the King-Size Shop, I have to scrounge around for hours, trying to find something I can get into, doesn't look like it was to wear for going out to get shot. Okay, you go down the Basement, you get the deals. I haven't got the time. I got to go to work and get the dough you spend onna deals."

"You could do it," she said. "Unusual sizes're very easy to find. Easier'n the stuff I'm looking for, that, everybody's got kids. It's just the same thing as the car, that's all. You don't want to. Money to spend on Jerry's just money, and Jerry's got it. Something his family needs, Jerry wants to know right off, how come and how much?"

"Where'd you learn this?" the Digger said. "You didn't know all these songs, I married you. I looked you over pretty good. I didn't hear nothing like this. Now you got that trap of yours working every minute. I wished I knew what the hell happened to you, made you different."

"Some things about you," she said, "changed a little in sixteen years. I used to be able to go to Confession."

"You still can," the Digger said. "Two blocks down, three over. It's a church thing, you'll recognize it right off. Course it don't sound the same, there's likely to be some hairy-looking bastard running around talking English like a Protestant, but it's right there. Every Saturday, Confessions three to five and seven to eight thirty, unless Father Alioto's got tickets to the ball game. Then seven to seven fifteen."

"I can't go to Confession," she said. "I can't tell them what we been doing."

"Oh for Christ sake," the Digger said, "wake up or something. Things've changed. Nobody pays any attention, that birth control thing. That's just the ghinny Pope raving around. Them guys, they must feel like they're running a drugstore, everybody coming in, one way or the other. They're used to hearing it."

"I'm not used to saying it," she said. "It'll bother *me*. What if he asks me, Jerry, what do I say?"

"Look him straight inna screen," the Digger said. "Tell him, 'The foam.' Then you say, 'What difference it make? My husband don't like the rubber boots, you take the Pill you're liable to grow a tail or something, and I ain't letting them put one of them things inside *me*. Then ask him, 'This how you get your cookies, Father? Asking people?' That'll slow him down."

45

"Of course I'll also be telling him," she said, "my great Catholic husband don't want any more children. Doesn't believe in sex for that any more. Just something he likes to do, like bowling or something."

"You can tell him that too," the Digger said. "Matter of fact, tell him I tried both and I think it over, I hadda give up one or the other, it'd be bowling. I see the ghinny Pope coming around with a couple hundred a week, the next kid to eat and wear and go to school on, and some more for a bigger house so I can do what I like to do without the whole goddamned world looking on, well then I'll say, 'Thanks, Pope,' and maybe we'll think about having another kid. Otherwise, my way."

"If you didn't spend every cent on yourself," she said, "we wouldn't need the extra. I know lots of families that haven't got anywhere near what you make, and they live much better. Their kids'er swimimng in the ocean this week. Our kids over the MDC pool. They go to the Cape, the kids go to camp, and my friends're all nicely dressed. I never have an extra dime, and when I do, you come back and take it. You and your wonderful friends, that's where the money goes. *You've* got the big convertible. *You're* going to the track. *You're* going to New York, to see the Giants. *We* can't afford twelve hundred dollars for *three weeks* at the Cape, but *you've* got a thousand dollars to go to Las Vegas. How much did you lose out there, Jerry, in four days by yourself?"

"All of it," the Digger said. "Just like you said."

"How much more did you lose?" she said.

"We been through all of this before," the Digger said. "I told you, I was taking a hundred bucks extra. I didn't bring no checks with me. That's all I took. So all right, I'm a bastard. Get off my back."

"Eleven hundred dollars," she said. "A hundred less'n we couldn't afford for three weeks. All on yourself. Oh, Jerry, I think that's selfish. I think that's very selfish. I thought it was the limit when you paid out a hundred and seventy dollars for the season's ticket to the Patriots, but at least that'll give you something for it. I would've been able to see it, even, if you'd got more of them so you could take the boys once in a while. But this, this is the worst thing you ever did, Jerry, the absolute worst thing."

"Good," the Digger said. "That's about the twentieth worst thing I remember. Now maybe you'll just howl about Vegas all the time and give me a change from the car and the clothes and all."

"Those were the worst until this one," she said. "Now you've topped them. I hope you don't think of a way to top this. I don't understand it. I never will. How could you come from the same mother and father as Paul, and be so different? So inconsiderate and mean. That, that I will never understand."

"Paul is a great guy," the Digger said. "I agree with you."

"Couldn't you," she said, "couldn't you just try to be more like him? Couldn't you do that?"

"Well," the Digger said, "I could. Course I'd have to get rid of you and them kids first, him being a priest and all, I don't think I could qualify. But I'll give it some thought, yeah."

"Think about us," she said. "Think about your family once in a while, instead of just yourself. What's happened to us, Jerry, think about that. If you figure it out, tell me, will you? Just tell me?"

The Digger stared at his coffee cup until after she had left the kitchen. "So far," he said to the cup, "so far it's really been a great day. I can hardly wait for the rest of it."

6

A TAN STUCCO WALL, eight feet high and capped with red tiles, shields the Church of the Holy Sepulchre from the noise of very light traffic on Larkspur Street in Weston. The driveway openings in the wall were built to accommodate LaSalles and Zephyrs.

Before noon the Digger eased the broad Oldsmobile through, reminding himself that he had managed the entrance before without gouging a fender.

The Digger parked at the edge of the oval drive, brushing the right fender with the heavy green foliage of the rhododendrons. Blood-colored hedge roses, pruned severely square, bloomed along the inside wall. Ponderous hydrangeas in white wooden tubs drooped before the roses. The air was crowded with fat honey-bees around the flowers. On the lawns an underground sprinkling system put up low, whispering fountains in the sunlight; a few corpulent robins walked in the spray, shaking their feathers now and then. In the shade of tall black maples at the end of the lawns, a silky silver Weimaraner arose and padded off toward the rear of the rectory. Keeping a close watch for bees, the Digger walked to the door of the stucco rectory, pushed the bell and sighed.

Mrs. Herlihy was about to turn sixty. She was gradually putting on flesh. She dressed in blue, simple suits, and might have been the hostess of a small tearoom known for its delicate pastries. Escorting the Digger toward the study she said again, "You could be twins."

48

In the study the Digger looked at the mutton-stripped, glass-front bookcases and the seven-foot, carved cherry desk. The carpet was a rose-colored Oriental; it took the sun nicely where the French doors opened on the flagstone terrace. At the corner of the terrace there were four potted rose trees; a small grey bird perched on one of them, and sang.

"I hate that woman," the Digger said, when Paul came into the study.

"Mrs. Herlihy?" Paul said. "I think the world of her. She runs the house perfectly. She has a very pleasant manner. I think sometimes we ought to ordain Mrs. Herlihy and let her take over the rest of the work. I haven't said that to Mrs. Herlihy."

"Every time I come here," the Digger said, "I got to tell her who I am. She knows who I am. Every time, after I tell her, she says we look like twins. She's jerking my chain. She don't like me."

"We look like twins because we both eat too much," Paul said. "But there're a lot of people who eat too much, and a lot of them come here. She can't be expected to remember every fat man's name, and you don't come here that often."

"I can see I should," the Digger said. "I could get used to this in a hurry. You still got the pool table in the cellar?"

"Billiard table," Paul said. "We're much too refined for pool. Of course." He wore a pale-yellow LaCoste sports shirt and white slacks. He wore white, slip-on shoes, no socks. "I don't generally move it out onto the lawn," he said.

"You had your hair cut," the Digger said. "It's different. It's, it's a different color. You're touching it up."

Paul sat in the tall, red leather chair behind the desk. "I had it cut in New York," he said. "I was there for a catechetical conference and I was staying at the Sherry Netherland. I needed a haircut so I had it cut. It's cut different from the way I usually have it cut."

"That could be," the Digger said. "But it's touched up, too. I got to hand it to you, Paul, you *look* like a Bishop. You live like a Bishop, too. Not bad at all."

"Supposed to be half the battle," Paul said. "When Father Celine brought the dog home, I told him he was giving himself and his ambitions away. Nobody short of a suffragan should have a dog like that. He said he likes to hunt."

"What does he hunt?" the Digger said. "Rich old ladies, I bet."

"No," Paul said, "he doesn't need to. Andy comes from the building Celines. He had a white Imperial convertible right out of the seminary, and his parents didn't have to throw him a parish-hall party to pay for it, either. He'll do all right."

"Everybody does all right," the Digger said. "I'm in the wrong line of work, is what I think."

"Oh come on," Paul said, "you do all right. A workingmen's bar in Dorchester? That's like a private gold mine. If Pa'd had something like that, he would've been in seventh heaven."

"He would've been in some kind of heaven," the Digger said, "and a lot sooner, too. Or else maybe down to the Washingtonian, drying out. He had enough trouble staying off the tea as it was. He hadda bar, I think he would've been pickled all the time. In addition to which, it's no soft touch, you know, things the way they are. New law now, we gotta serve broads. Guys don't like it, guys' wives don't like it, I agree with them: booze and broads don't mix. Also, I got to put in another toilet, which is going to run me a good three thousand before I'm through and I lose space too. Time I get it, it'll be time for Father Finn's regular sermon about the evils of drink, and that'll fall the trade off for a week or two. It's no picnic, Paul."

"I could speak to Father Finn, if you want," Paul said.

"I'd rather you didn't," the Digger said. "It gets Aggie upset and all, and it cost me money, but it also don't encourage anybody else, thinking about going to the Licensing for another joint. Ask him instead, how he liked the ghinny Assistant."

"Still your old tolerant self, I see, Jerry," Paul said.

"I been around," the Digger said, "I work hard, I

50

seen a few things. I can think what I want. I don't like ghinnies, is all. I got reasons."

"Heaven's going to be hard for you," Paul said. "They're nowhere near as selective as you are, from what I hear."

"Yeah," the Digger said, "I heard that too. I didn't hear it from Father Finn, of course, but I see Alioto's working around to that every so often. Coons and everything. Course that's only true if there's anything to the rest of it, shade just doesn't go down and that's the end of you."

"You're not sure?" Paul said.

"Put it this way," the Digger said, "if they got that thing and all, it's not crowded. I sure don't know that many guys I'd expect to find there."

"You expect to get the chance to look, though," Paul said.

"Well," the Digger said, "there was Ma. Now Ma, she did what she was supposed to do, and she laid off the other stuff, and she put up with Pa and me. So, and that other thing, she had a son a priest, which is the free ticket, the way I get it. So, it's all true, Ma is okay. Now me, I figure the one chance I got is to kick off when it's raining, no golf, a weekday, say in April, no ball game, middle of the afternoon so you already had your nap. I see it coming, I'm gonna say, 'Aggie, gimme the chaplain, baby. Call over to Saint Hilary's, Father Finn ain't in, try the Lutherans and then the Jews. Worst comes to worst, the black fella down in the store Columbus Ave, under the el.' Because that's the only chance I got, somebody comes by when I'm too weak to get in any more trouble and wipes it all off, says, 'Let him in, God. He made it.' Ma, Ma could've died in a closet when the Broons're playing Canadiens, there isn't a priest for miles. She still would've been all right. Maureen's inna convent. She goes and they say, 'Let her in, works for the Boss.' Kathy? Kathy married the Corola wine company. Either she goes straight to hell for marrying the wop or she goes straight to heaven for living with the wop, I forget which Ma finally decided. Either way, nothing she can do about it. You got the retirement plan. Me, I gotta be realistic. I go at a time when I can't get the house call, I'm sunk."

"Does it bother you?" Paul said.

"Yeah," the Digger said, "a little."

"Enough to do something about it?" Paul said.

"No," the Digger said, "not enough for that. I figure, I make it, great. They gotta, there's gotta be some reason, they call it Paradise. I don't make it, it's there to be had, well, too bad, at least I'll see all my friends in the other place. And if there isn't no place, either kind, well, at least I didn't waste no time worrying about it."

"I think that's a healthy attitude," Paul said.

"Yeah," the Digger said.

"I do," Paul said. "It's not that far off from mine. The way I look at it, I'm telling people what I really believe to be true. But maybe it isn't true. All right. If they do what I tell them, and it's true, I've done a lot of good. That makes me feel good. If they do what I tell them, and it isn't true, what've they lost? There's nothing wrong with the model of Christian life, even if there isn't any jackpot at the end. It's an orderly, dignified way to live, and that's not a bad thing."

"I don't think that's what Ma thought you were up to when you got ordained, there," the Digger said.

"I'm sure it wasn't," Paul said. "Ma was a good, simple woman. I don't think it's what *I* was up to, when I got ordained."

"That's nice talk," the Digger said.

"I didn't mean anything," Paul said. "I mean it: she knew what she believed in, and she believed in it. I'd give a great deal today for a church full of people like her. I offer Mass at least twice a week, for the repose of her soul."

"Now there's something I could use," the Digger said, "a little of that repose of the soul. That'd be just the item."

"Well," Paul said, "you had yourself a little excursion a week or so ago. Things can't be that bad."

"How'd you hear that?" the Digger said.

"I ran into Aggie," Paul said. "I had some business at the Chancery and then I took the trolley intown and went to see Father Francis at the Shrine, take him to lunch. Aggie was coming out when I went in. She had Patricia with her. Those are beautiful children, my nephews and niece, even if I am their uncle."

"I wonder what the hell she was doing in there," the Digger said. "She didn't tell me she was intown."

"You were away," Paul said. "I suppose she figured, well, the cat's away. Here's my chance to get roaring drunk. So, naturally, she stopped in at the Shrine with your daughter to get things off to a proper start. She said you were out in Las Vegas and she was in shopping and stopped in at the Shrine to say a prayer for your safe return. Nothing sinister about that, is there?"

"No," the Digger said, "I didn't mean that. I just didn't know she was in there, is all. She can do what she likes."

"How'd you happen to be in Las Vegas?" Paul said.

"Oh, you know," the Digger said, "one thing and another. I know this guy, he's inna travel business, he had this deal, he had some room onna plane and did me and some of the guys want to go. So, you know, we hear a lot about Vegas, yeah, we'll go. So, you pay five bucks, you join this club, then they can give you the plane fare, practically for nothing. They got this kind of a special deal with the hotel, so, really, it's pretty cheap, you do it that way. It's almost all the way across the country and all. You get your meals, couple of drinks, you can play golf. I played golf. It's really a pretty good deal."

"You like Vegas, huh?" Paul said.

"It's pretty hot," the Digger said. "During the day it was awful hot. See, that's one of the reasons you can get the rate, going out this time of year. It's so hot, a lot of people don't want to go. So the hotels, you know, they pay part of it. But it was still hot. One of the days it got up to a hundred and fifteen. I wouldn't want to live there. I just wanted to see what it was like."

"Of course the main attraction's the gambling," Paul said.

"Well, but they have a lot of big-name entertainment there too," the Digger said.

"Who'd you see?" Paul said.

"It was kind of funny, actually," the Digger said. "I was going to, they had this opera fellow that was supposed to sing there, Mario Lanza?"

"Mario Lanza's been dead about ten years," Paul said.

"Must've been somebody else, then," the Digger said. "Like I say, I forget his name. Anyway, he was sick. Nero. Franco Nero?"

"The only one I ever heard of," Paul said, "was Corelli. I doubt he sings out there."

"I dunno," the Digger said. "Whoever it was, he was sick. So they just had, it was some guys I never heard of. They had a comedian and they had this floor show and a guy sang popular."

"What was the floor show, Jerry?" Paul said.

"Gee," the Digger said, "well, you know, it was a *floor* show."

"I don't know," Paul said. "Tell me about it. What am I missing?"

"Well," the Digger said, "they had these dance numbers. They had these girls come out in the headdresses and all, and then they got this number, they wheel out a big glass staircase, you know? And the girls come out and they stand on it."

"They just stand on it?" Paul said. "People pay money to see that?"

"Paul," the Digger said, "they don't have any clothes on."

"*Okay,*" Paul said. "Now, that I can understand. I've got a couple friends in the parish that go to Las Vegas from time to time, and they're the kind of men that I would imagine probably get around a little. And they've invited me to go, and of course I've always said, 'No.' I don't think the Bishop'd like it. Well, they think that means I disapprove of *them* going, and actually, I guess I do. Although they can well afford it, whatever it costs. But that means I never get to hear what it is that I missed. I just wanted to know what it is that I don't think the Bishop'd want me to see, whatever it is."

"You can't actually see that much," the Digger said. "I was sitting away back in the place, you know?

They were naked, I could see that. But otherwise, nothing much."

"That's from being a regular churchgoer," Paul said. "You're so used to sitting at the back so you can leave early, you just automatically sit at the back, now. Your old habits're too much for you. Did you by any chance do some gambling, Jerry?"

"Well, yeah," the Digger said, "I did some gambling."

"How much gambling did you do?" Paul said.

"Now look," the Digger said, "gambling, you know, I done it before. I know where Suffolk is, the Rock, Gansett. I even bet onna baseball game now and then. I didn't, I know about gambling, Paul. I didn't have to go all the way out to Vegas to gamble."

"Well, that's true, of course," Paul said. "Did you win or lose?"

"I lost," the Digger said.

"You lost," Paul said.

"Look," the Digger said, "I'm not one of them guys comes around and he's always telling you, he won. People lose, gambling. I lost."

"That's why they run gambling, I think," Paul said. "People lose their money at it."

"Mostly," the Digger said, "mostly, they do."

"How much did you lose, Jerry?" Paul said.

"Well," the Digger said, "if it's all the same to you, I'd just as soon not go into it."

"Jerry," Paul said, "I'd love not to go into it. You got a deal."

There was an extended silence. There was a ship's clock on the mantel of the fireplace in the study of the rectory of the Church of the Holy Sepulchre. It had a soft tick, inaudible except in near-absolute silence. It ticked several times.

"How's your car running?" the Digger said.

"I've been thinking of turning it in," Paul said.

"Something the matter with it?" the Digger said. His face showed concern. "Car's not that old, you don't drive it all the time. It's, what, a six-thousand-dollar item? Oughta be all right for five years or so."

"It's two years old," Paul said. "Nineteen thousand miles on it. There's nothing wrong with it. I was just

55

thinking, I might trade it. I always wanted a Cadillac."

"Those're *nice,*" the Digger said. "I wouldn't mind one of them myself. I see one a while back, had a real close look at it. Really a nice car."

"Yeah," Paul said. "But I can't buy a Cadillac. The parishioners, they wouldn't mind. Most of them have Cadillacs themselves. But Billy Maloney, sold me the Buick, he'd be angry. And Billy's a good friend of mine. Then there's the Chancery. They wouldn't like it. You buy yourself a Cadillac, in a way it's sort of like saying, 'I've got all I want.' At least they're not going to give you any more, and that's about the same thing. I can't have a Cadillac. But then I started looking at those Limiteds."

"That's another nice car," the Digger said.

"And it's still a Buick," Paul said, "so it won't get anybody's nose out of joint. But it's the closest thing to a Cadillac that I've seen so far."

"What do they go for?" the Digger said.

"Bill treats me all right," Paul said. "This'll be the fourth car I've bought from him. I suppose, twenty-eight hundred and mine."

"He's using you all right," the Digger said. "That's an eight-thousand-dollar unit, I figure, you get it all loaded up. You do all right, Big Brother."

"Around seventy-four hundred, actually," Paul said. "My one indulgence, you know?"

The Digger looked around the room. "Yup," he said, "right. Cottage. In the winter, Florida. Didn't Aggie tell me something about, you're going to Ireland in a month or so?"

"October," Paul said. "Leading a pilgrimage. Something like your Las Vegas thing, I suppose. Except Lourdes is supposed to be the highlight, no naked women and no gambling. Just holy water. Then you get to come back through Ireland and get what really interests you, the Blarney Stone and that idiocy they put on at Bunratty Castle. All that race-of-kings stuff."

"Gee," the Digger said, "I would've thought the types out here'd be too fine for that, all that jigging around."

"They are," Paul said. "You couldn't sell a tour in this parish if you put up *ten* plenary indulgences. In the summer, God bless them, the envelopes come in from Boothbay and Cataumet. The ones that aren't all tanned in February, from taking the kids to Saint Thomas, are all tanned from taking the kids to Mount Snow. This is for Monsignor Fahey's parish, Saint Malachy's in Randolph. He set it up. Then his doctor told him he'd prefer the Monsignor didn't travel around too much until everybody's sure the pacemaker's working all right. So Monsignor Fahey asked me to take it. Well, he was my first pastor, and he still gets a respectful hearing at the Chancery. I'll do the man a favor."

"Look," the Digger said, "speaking of favors. I got a problem I was hoping maybe you could help me out with."

"Sure," Paul said.

"Well, I didn't tell you yet," the Digger said.

"I meant: of course you have," Paul said.

"I don't get it," the Digger said.

"Jerry," Paul said, "am I stupid? Do you think I'm stupid?"

"God, no," the Digger said. "You had, what was it, college and then you're in the seminary all that time. You went over to Rome there, you even went to college summers. Now you got all this. No, I don't think that."

"Good," Paul said.

"I never had any education like that," the Digger said.

"Because you weren't interested," Paul said. "Not interested enough to do what you had to, to get it."

"Well," the Digger said, "I mean, you wanted to be a priest. I thought Ma was always saying that's something you get from God. You don't just wake up inna morning and say, 'What the hell, nothing to do today, guess I'll be a priest.' "

"You could've done it other ways," Paul said. "You could've finished school in the service. You could've finished school when you were in school, instead of being in such a hurry to be a wise guy that you couldn't bother."

"I hated school," the Digger said.

"Right," Paul said. "That's what I'm saying. Nobody handed me anything I've got."

"I didn't mean that," the Digger said. "You earned it. I know that."

"I don't," Paul said, "I dont know any such thing. I think I lucked out. I was in the right place at the right time, two or three times."

"That's just as good," the Digger said.

"It's better," Paul said, "I'll take it any time. My problem wasn't getting it. My problem was keeping it after I got it. That problem is you."

"Now just a goddamned minute," the Digger said.

"Take two if you like," Paul said, "they're small. I've been here eight years. Eight years since Monsignor Labelle got so far into his dotage nobody could pretend any more, and they put me in as administrator. That was in November. He was still alive in December, when Patricia was christened. After Christmas."

"I thought we might get into that again," the Digger said. "Funny thing. I did time and then I come out and I never been in trouble again. Governor even give me a piece of paper, everything's fair and square. But the other thing, I guess that's gonna go on for the rest of forever, that right?"

"Keep in mind how you got to be such buddies with the Governor," Paul said. "And if you want to bring up that Christmas when I was Uncle Father and Daddy both, you can go ahead. I didn't plan to."

"I made a mistake," the Digger said. "I admit it. I didn't think it's a mistake at the time. Now I know. Move over, Hitler."

"Come off it, Jerry," Paul said.

"Come off it yourself," the Digger said. "Big deal. I went to a football game. The State'd forget about it by now, they couldn't prove after eight years I went to a football game and it was a crime. I think probably even Aggie forgot about it by now."

"She'll never forget," Paul said.

"You guys," the Digger said, "you guys know more about women on less practice than anything I ever see. You want to know something? That celibacy

58

thing, I hope you get what you're after, stop a lot of this pious horseshit about family life we been getting every Sunday ever since I can remember. Serve you guys right."

"Aggie's a fine human being," Paul said.

"She is," the Digger said. "You never saw a better one. But the Blessed Virgin Mary she's not. You ask me, the Blessed Virgin Mary probably wasn't what you guys always seem to go around thinking she was. Stomp around the garden reading the black book every day, you get so's you think that's what it is. Well, it's not. It's what somebody, lived a long time ago, wrote to cover up what he knew and what he thought people oughta be, and they aren't."

"We hear confessions, too," Paul said.

"Yeah," the Digger said, "and who goes? Little kids, didn't drink their orange juice."

The clock ticked several times.

"You always did have an instinct for the jugular," Paul said.

"I always done the best I could," the Digger said. "Nobody ever bought me a car, I was getting set to go out and hold hands with old ladies."

"Now look," Paul said.

"Now look nothing," the Digger said. "Aggie and me, we get along all right. She don't think I'm perfect. She's right. I don't think she's perfect, either, and she ain't. We're a couple of people and sometimes what we do, it doesn't turn out right. But we get along."

"So," Paul said, "she had your baby and then you couldn't make Christmas because you wanted to go down to Miami. That was a mean thing to do."

"It was," the Digger said. "Eight years later, I see it now. I had it thrown up to me enough. I asked her, she mind if I went to the football game. 'No.' I go. All right, I knew she didn't like it. But I figure, she don't, it don't make her mad enough to *say* she don't like it. So I go. Then she gets a whole lot of backer-uppers like you and I get more shit about that game'n I get for stolen goods. The judge was easier on me, and he put me in jail. At least that ended some time."

"I tell you what," Paul said, "let's act like adults. The game was Kitty Lee. Forget the charming story

59

about the game, all right? Aggie never believed it anyway. I did, but I'm naïve. I was naïve. I believed you."

"Well," the Digger said, "we went to the game."

"Sure," Paul said. "Then in February I had Monsignor Labelle in the ground and I was trying to get this shop on an even keel again. Trying very hard because I'd been a priest sixteen years and this was the first parish I really wanted. Thirty-eight years old, and a prize in my hands if I didn't mess it up. And you showed up."

"I did," the Digger said.

"Yeah," Paul said. "Kitty was a year shy of the age of consent when you went off to that game with her, and the Chinese family didn't take to that kind of mistake, did it, Jerry?"

"The old man was a little pissed," the Digger said.

"That's a very handy way of putting it," Paul said. "He'd been to the District Attorney, in fact. So I had to call Eddie Gaffney down at Saint Pius and get him to speak to somebody who knew the Assistant D.A. on the case. And I also had to explain to Eddie why it was that my half-witted brother, whom he'd gotten a pardon for, out of the goodness of his heart, was in trouble again."

"Somebody got a thousand dollars for that pardon, I remember it," the Digger said. "I think it might've been Goodness Gaffney's goddamned lawyer brother up to the State House there, was the fellow, I think about it long enough."

"Jerry," Paul said, "a lawyer represents you, he gets a fee."

"Somebody else does," the Digger said, "it's a bribe they call it."

"I call it a fee," Paul said. "Since I paid it, I think I ought to get to call it what I like. I thought that was all it was going to take to set you up, so I wouldn't have to worry about you any more. Then Kitty Lee came along, and I was in for it again. It was harder that time. The Lees were mad, and they were, what were they, anyway, Jerry, Congregationalists?"

"Some kind of Protestants," the Digger said.

"Congregationalists," Paul said. "Eddie Gaffney had to call Father Wang. Father Wang called the Reverend Doctor Wong. Doctor Wong seriously exaggerated your contrition to the Lees. Where the hell did you meet Kitty Lee, anyway?"

"Inna bar," the Digger said. "I was down to the Saratoga, there, she come in with a couple of guys I knew. I scooped her. She was a cute kid."

"That was a great idea, Jerry," Paul said.

"I know," the Digger said. "I should've asked to see her license."

"Five thousand dollars for not asking," Paul said.

"I thought that was steep at the time," the Digger said.

"I didn't," Paul said. "If Mister Lee'd wanted twenty, I would've given it to him. Statutory rape. Mann Act. Great stuff for me, Jerry. Five thousand was cheap. Dirty, but cheap."

"It was still high for hush money," the Digger said.

"Maybe," Paul said, "but it was my check. It was my money. I knew I wasn't going to get it back. If I'd've thought you could get five thousand dollars together in a bank vault with a rake, I might've asked you. As it was, I took Mister Lee's offer before he changed his mind."

"Half of it was mine anyway," the Digger said.

"Half of what?" Paul said. "Half of what was yours?"

"The five," the Digger said. "I'm not knocking you. I appreciated what you did. But half that five, that should've been mine anyway. The rest, the rest was yours."

"From what?" Paul said.

"The Hibernian insurance," the Digger said. "Ma had five from the Hibernians, she died. You got it all."

"I was the beneficiary," Paul said.

"Sure," the Digger said, "and she's inna rest home, I went over there every goddamned morning before I go down the place, I stop at the store first and I buy her a pack of Luckies and the paper. Rain or shine, and I talk to her at least an hour. I think I missed once, the whole eight months she was there. I had the runs and I couldn't get as far away from the toilet as it would've

61

taken me to drive there. I got hell for that, too. Listen to her, day after day, bitching about the way they treat her, they treated her *good*. That's a good home. 'What am I doing here, you'd think I didn't have a family,' all the rest of it. Every damned day."

"I know," Paul said, "I caught some of that too."

"I got a seven-room house," the Digger said. "I'm a good Catholic, I got four young kids. Two oldest in one room and Patricia and Matthew in the other one, she keeps him up all night with the crying, makes him cranky as hell all the time, she was just a little kid. They were both little kids, and Aggie's taking care of both of them, she's not getting no sleep, I got to listen to Ma. Where am I supposed to put her? She started in on me one day, I was up late and I guess probably I was a little hard on her. 'Ma,' I said, 'you can sleep inna goddamned yard, all right? No, I'll do better'n that for you. The garage, put a nice cot there. Beat the hell out of the car, but, and I got to warn you, might be a little chilly this time of year. Better wait till she warms up some. Then you can come and live inna garage, all right? Wait till May.' She got all pissed off, hollering and yelling, raised me from a pup, she wallops the pots over to the Poor Clares, this and that, now she's old and sick. Jesus, it was awful."

"I know," Paul said, "I got some of it too."

"Well," the Digger said, "where the hell're you gonna put her? You're over to Saint Stephen's then. You put her inna tabernacle, maybe?"

"Not me," Paul said, "I could do no wrong. You."

"Oh," the Digger said, "beautiful. I was also getting it when I wasn't even around."

"She was a querulous old woman," Paul said. "She had a lot of pain. She was immobile, and she'd always done for herself. She was sick."

"And when she died," the Digger said, "she had five thousand bucks which she didn't leave to me."

"Look," Paul said, "I'll add some things up. If you want, when I get through, I'll split down the middle with you, all right?"

"Deal," the Digger said.

"Coughlin nailed me fourteen hundred dollars for Ma's funeral," Paul said. "Twenty months before, eleven hundred for Pa's. I paid it. I looked him right in the eye. I said, 'You know, Johnny, I thought eleven was pretty high when I settled for my father. This was almost the identical funeral, same casket and everything. I think fourteen hundred's a little steep.'

" 'I know it,' he said, in that oily voice he used when he's giving you the business," Paul said, " 'but I can't help it, Monsignor, to save myself. Everything's going up all the time. I just can't keep up with it. I sympathize with you, believe me. This is rock-bottom.'

" 'Calling me "Monsignor" doesn't ease the pain, Coughlin,' I said," Paul said, "and I paid him. That was the last time Coughlin saw anything the archdiocese had to hand out. That was the most expensive fourteen-hundred-dollar funeral that devil ever ran, I can guarantee you that."

"I thought Dad's insurance covered his funeral," the Digger said.

"It did," Paul said. "He had five with the Hibernians, too. A thousand from the union. Social Security was a little over two hundred."

"So that didn't come out of you," the Digger said.

"Sorry," Paul said. "I got the canceled check for his funeral, if you'd like to see it. The insurance went to Ma. I never asked her for it. She had nothing else. No Social Security from the Poor Clares, no retirement either. That insurance was all she had."

"Bastards," the Digger said.

"If they had it," Paul said, "guys like you'd have to pay for it. Since they don't, guys like me have to pay for it. No complaint: the Church didn't treat Ma like it should've, and that was bad, but it treated me a lot better'n it probably should've, and I took it. So she washed the floor and she walked on it and she slipped and she broke her hip. How many years'd she done that?"

"Ever since I can remember," the Digger said.

"Sure," Paul said, "you take it in stride. The hospital was thirty-three hundred dollars that I paid, *plus* whatever she paid."

"Hey," the Digger said.

"That was before the nursing home," Paul said. "Flynn runs a good home, as you say. He also charges all outdoors. In two months of drugs and special nurses and the man who cuts toenails she sent right through all the money in the bank that I hadn't asked her for. Then I started writing checks again. Every week, two-fifty-three, two-fifty-seven, two-fifty-six. I figure, thirty-five hundred dollars or so. Okay, want half?"

"No," the Digger said.

"You're sure," Paul said. "Eleven for Pa's funeral, fourteen for hers, thirty-five hundred for her being sick, in the home, plus the thirty-three I paid the hospital, you sure you don't want half of the Hibernians?"

"I didn't know," the Digger said. "I figured, Ma's probably pissed off at me, I went inna can. I didn't know you spent all that dough."

"What is it you want, Jerry?" Paul said.

"Money," the Digger said.

"That," Paul said, "that, I know. When Aggie told me where you were, I went inside the Shrine and offered up a prayer. Before I saw Father Francis. I asked God to grant you a safe return. I also asked Him to keep you out of games you couldn't afford. I even asked Him to let you win. I was praying for me. I said, 'God, you're not paying attention. He's going to get in trouble. Please get him out.' "

"Father Doherty," the Digger said, "I got some bad news for you about the power of prayers."

"How much?" Paul said.

"Eighteen thousand dollars," the Digger said.

The ship's clock ticked several times.

"That," Paul said, "is a very impressive sum of money."

"I think so," the Digger said. "I know I was impressed. I didn't really know, you know, how bad it was. Then I get back to the room, and I add everything up. Well, I had an idea. But I add it up, I was, I was impressed. I felt like somebody kicked me in the guts, is how I felt."

The clock ticked several more times.

"I can understand that," Paul said. "Of course the question is, where're you going to get the money?"

"Well," the Digger said, "I *got* some of it."

"How much?" Paul said.

"About two thousand," the Digger said.

"That leaves you sixteen thousand to get," Paul said.

"That's the way it come out when I did the figuring onna way over here," the Digger said.

"Where do you plan to get it?" Paul said.

"I been running a little short of ideas," the Digger said. "I know where to get sixteen, but it's probably gonna get me in a deep tub of shit. That's why I come out here. That don't appeal to me. Now you say, you remind me, all them times I come out here, I'm inna bind. Right. But I don't *like* asking you, you know? I know you're pretty sick of it. I'm a big pain in the ass. But it isn't, I don't *plan* all them things, you know? I just got a way, it seems like I can stay out of trouble just so long, and then there I am, in trouble again. And here I am again. I had some way, getting that dough, Paul, I wouldn't be here. But I don't. I haven't got any way of getting it, won't get me in worse trouble'n I am in already."

"Who," Paul said, "to whom do you owe all this money? Forgive me, I'm innocent. Is it some casino? I never knew anybody in a scrape like this."

"Well," the Digger said, "actually, probably, I don't know yet. Some loan shark."

"Fellow in a black sedan," Paul said, "cigar."

"Could be," the Digger said. "I know one, looks like that. But see, I don't know who's got the markers, yet. I thought somebody'd be in before this. I still owe it. It's some shy."

"How much time will he let you have," Paul said, "to raise this money?"

"Time?" the Digger said. "He'll let me have the rest of my life, is what he'll let me have. That's the way he wants it. It's me, I don't want the time. I figure the vig goes me four and five hundred. Probably five, maybe I hold him off for four, it's somebody it turns out I know."

"Four hundred dollars a month," Paul said.

"Four hundred a *week*," the Digger said. "I got two grand. That's either vig plus sixteen off the nut, or it's five weeks to raise the eighteen. See, that's what I come out here, find out, what do I do, what do I plan on? I dunno how I use the two."

"Say it," Paul said.

"Say what?" the Digger said.

"Say what you want me to do," Paul said. "Those other times I listened to your story and then I said I'd try to help you, and you said: 'Thanks,' and I started making telephone calls and presuming on friendships, trying to find a way out for you. This time I want you to say right out what you want me to do. I think it might do you good to hear yourself say it."

"I want you to give me sixteen thousand dollars," the Digger said.

"Not *lend*," Paul said, "*give*."

"Paul," the Digger said, "if I could borrow sixteen, if I could go somewhere and get it, I wouldn't be here. No, I admit it, I didn't come here, I'm not looking for no loan."

"You want me to give you sixteen thousand dollars," Paul said, "just like that. Sixteen thousand dollars."

"Yeah," the Digger said.

"No," Paul said.

The clock ticked.

The Digger cleared his throat. "Paul," he said, "you know, maybe you don't know, you know what this means. It don't matter, what shy got the paper, you know? They all work the same way. They're going to come around and say, where's the money? And I got to have the money for him, is all. Otherwise, well, they got, every one of them has got a guy or so with a Louisville Slugger, come around and break your kneecaps for you or something. I mean that, Paul. I could get my knees broken."

"I believe it," Paul said. "You convinced me, a long long time ago, that if anybody knows how those things're done, you do."

"Paul," the Digger said, "I don't like the idea, you know? Getting the knees busted up, it don't appeal to me."

"I'm sure it doesn't," Paul said.

"Furthermore," the Digger said, "furthermore, I'm not *getting* the knees broke. That's how much it don't appeal to me: I'm not gonna sit around and wait for it to happen. I'm gonna do something before it happens."

"That seems to have a threatening sound to it," Paul said.

"You can take it any way you want," the Digger said. "One way or the other, I'm getting that dough. You don't give it to me, I'm getting it some other way. But I am getting it. I don't need the kind of grief a man gets if he don't."

"Well, now," Paul said, "let's see. There aren't an awful lot of ways you can do that. Seems to me as though about the only thing you can do is go to a bank and get yourself a mortgage man."

"That's one of the first things I think of," the Digger said. "I can hock the Bright Red. Then I think, I'll be lucky, somebody'll give me ten onna place. So that means: the house, I got to hock the house. What's that good for? I suppose I could probably get five onna house, I was to go out and look for it. So, I'm still short, and not only that, what's Aggie got then? Nothing. So I think, I say, I'm gonna do it. It's not Aggie and the kids' fault, I need that kind of dough. It's something I did. I can't go out and do that to them. I gotta keep them things free."

"Very touching," Paul said. "Of course it doesn't leave you much room to maneuver, but there it is."

"There it is," the Digger said. "I'm not looking for no credit, Paul. I'm just telling you, I'm not getting no more mortgages. So that leaves me, that leaves me with some of the other things I think of to do."

"Which are?" Paul said.

"Well," the Digger said, "I don't know as I oughta answer you that one. See, some of them could be kind of risky, and you might get nervous."

"Now that," Paul said, "that is very definitely a threat. As little as I know about being threatened, I can recognize that. Just what do you plan to do, Jerry? Rob the poor box down at Saint Hilary's?"

"What I got planned," the Digger said, "it's none of your business, Paul. You don't want to help? Okay, you don't want to help. I give you credit, you lay it right onna line. You don't gimme the long face and say, 'Jeez, Jerry, I don't have it.' Man knows where he stands with you, at least. Until the kneecaps go, anyway."

"I have got it," Paul said.

"There you go," the Digger said, "of course you got it. You got the fancy dogs running around and the hair, dyeing the hair, the whole bit. The rugs, you got to have it. That's why I come to you. But I give you credit, you don't shit a man. I ask you and you say, 'Fuck you.' Okay, fuck me. But I give you that, you put it right down there, no bullshit about old Paul. Way to go, Paul *baby*. Course they're not your kneecaps, but that don't matter, does it."

"Oh come off it, Jerry," Paul said. "None of this belongs to me and you know it. It all belonged to Labelle before me, and it'll belong to somebody else after me. None of this is mine, Jerry."

"But you're still all right, right, Paul?" the Digger said. "Long as Paul's all right, that's all that matters."

"The car's mine," Paul said. "The clothes're mine. I've got a couple of very small bank accounts, when you think about how long I've had to work to get them. I couldn't live two years on what I've got in the bank. The rest belongs to the Church."

"You got the place at Onset," the Digger said.

"I have," Paul said. "I paid fifteen-five for that place seven years ago. I've reduced the principal considerably since then, mostly by putting money into it that I might've liked to spend on something else. It's about twenty-eight thousand now, with appreciation and inflation and the improvements I've made. I owe three thousand on the note, now. So, in equity, I've got twenty-five thousand dollars, say. About that."

"That's what I was saying," the Digger said.

"Those things," Paul said, "American Express'll trust me for a month and I've got a new set of Walter Hagens. I've got five thousand dollars' worth of AT and T. I spent twenty-four years of my life grubbing up that very little pile. If I retire at sixty-five, the way I expect I'll have to when I get to be sixty-five, I've got nineteen years left to add to it. If I can stay on till I'm seventy, or don't die or something before

68

then, I'm precisely halfway along. Otherwise, I'm on the decline.

"Now, what is it you want, Jerry?" Paul said. "You want those twenty-four years to pay for three or four days of you making a goddamned ass of yourself. That's what your position is. You're forty-two years old and you're still acting like you never grew up, and you expect me to pay for it. You want me to turn over everything I've got, to you, and start over. I won't do it.

"That house in Onset is my retirement home. I've got to pay it off before I get on a pension, because I won't be able to carry more than the taxes when I retire. Maybe not even those. I'd better not live too long, is what I'm saying. If I mortgage it now, I pay off some bookies in Nevada, I won't have it when I quit. I just won't. I'll have to sell it and throw the money into the common pot of some home for drooling old priests and spend the rest of my years getting chivvied about by jovial nuns. No thanks. This time you want more'n I can afford."

"I'm sorry I came," the Digger said.

"You're nowhere near as sorry as I am," Paul said. "That doesn't mean I'm not sorry you got yourself into this mess, though. Now, you told me what you wanted me to do, and I told you I won't do it. And you're mad. If you're interested, I'll tell you what I will do, and you can take it or leave it. If you'd rather be mad, you can be mad. Suit yourself."

The Digger had started to get up. He sat down again. "I'm desperate," he said, "I'll take anything."

"Oh, I know that," Paul said, "but this is a little more than that, taking something. This is a deal. A deal, you have to give up something, am I right?"

"Yup," the Digger said.

"I'll give you my Limited," Paul said. "I've got three thousand dollars in a special bank account, what I got for Christmas and Easter and baptisms and weddings over the past few years. There isn't going to be any more of that now, the pastor's special get-rich-slow scheme, but that's the way it goes. The Electra's good for at least another year, and my Limited's probably not as important to me as your knee-caps are to you. Or to me, for that matter.

"Now," Paul said, "you can do whatever you like with the money. You can buy seven more weeks, of whatever it is, or you can reduce the principal. Just as I did on my house. It's completely up to you."

"I'm not hocking the place," the Digger said.

"Jerry," Paul said, "I'm not asking you to do any-thing. I'm telling you something. You can have three thousand dollars, free, gratis and for nothing. You don't have to pay it back."

"But I got to do something," the Digger said.

"Correct," Paul said. "I get your solemn word: this is the last time. You're my brother, but you're a little old now to need a keeper, and I've had my share of the job. I don't want it any more. I never had much luck at it anyway.

"I don't ask for miracles, Jerry," Paul said. "They're nice, but they're hard to come by. You'll be in another mess next year. You know it and I know it. I don't want promises of good behavior."

"Okay," the Digger said.

"What I want," Paul said, "what I want is peace and quiet. I want a promise that you'll go to someone else, the next time you get in the soup. You won't even *tell* me about it."

"Okay," the Digger said.

"I'm not finished," Paul said. "I'm at the point where a man has to drive a hard bargain. I should've done it before, but I didn't. Now I've got to, or you'll just keep on coming back until you beggar me.

"You started talking about risky things," Paul said. "I know your history. You went to prison for mind-ing Dinny Hand's cellar full of stolen jewelry, twenty years ago, and you didn't learn a solitary thing. You almost went to prison when they found out about those television sets and stereos in the cellar of the Bright Red. It was all I could do to persuade them the help put them in there and you didn't know about it, and you know I was lying, Jerry, and I knew it too. Your vacation was all that saved you, that time, that and the silence of your friends.

"I know the way your mind works," Paul said. "I

don't like it, but I know it. When you get the chance, you steal. The trouble is that you're not a very good thief. You've been caught twice. The last time you were next door to a long sentence. You got away that time. You won't get away again. You see, I know them, too, from dealing with them in your behalf. They remember a man who got one free. If he slips again, they land on him."

"Just out of curiosity," the Digger said, "what do you care, this is the write-off and all? I don't mean nothing by it, I'm just asking."

"I've been here two years short of the magic number," Paul said. "Nobody's ever been pastor of Holy Sepulchre for ten years without making domestic prelate. I'd like to, Jerry, I'd really like to. I'd like for you not to foul it up for me."

"That's what I thought," the Digger said.

"What you think is your business," Paul said. "Your family deserves something better'n weekends traveling back and forth to Walpole to see Daddy. I deserve something better'n coming downstairs every year to hear about Little Brother's latest calamity. You tell me you won't mortgage the house or the saloon to get the money that you lost all by yourself. But there's no other legal way to get it. So you're telling me you'll commit crimes. And I'm telling you, you'll get caught. Don't give me that pious stuff about your family. I'll give you three thousand dollars. For that I get your promises: no more emergency visits, *and no more crimes*. You'll get caught."

"You're buying me off," the Digger said.

"I'm buying me," Paul said, "I'm buying *me* off. I told you. I'm making provision for my old age. I'm through bailing you out. Now I'm buying me off. I want those assurances. For three thousand dollars, we're quits. Take it or leave it."

"Take it," the Digger said.

"I've got your word," Paul said.

"You got my word," the Digger said.

"On both things," Paul said.

"On both things," the Digger said.

"I'd better have," Paul said. "I was really looking forward to that Limited."

71

7

"JESUS *Christ*, DIG," the Greek said, "you've got way in over your fuckin' *head*. I saw that fuckin' marker, I almost fuckin' *shit*. The fuck's the matter with you, you lose your fuckin' *mind* or something? Guys, guys like us, you haven't got that kind of fuckin' money. What the fuck happened?"

"You'd make some guy a great fuckin' wife, you know that, Greek?" the Digger said. "That fuckin' mouth of yours, come inna my place and start playing it like it was a fuckin' radio, anybody ask you to do that? Fuck you, Greek."

"Fuck you, Dig," the Greek said. They sat at a table at the rear of the Bright Red. They had draught beers in front of them. It was early in the afternoon and the air conditioner made a steady white ripple of interference across the ball game on the television set above the front door. "That's my fuckin' eighteen K you're getting so fuckin' big about. It was your eighteen, you had eighteen K, I might come around and be nice. But it's my paper and I know fuckin' well you haven't got the dough and that makes you a big fuckin' *problem*. Them I don't like."

"Look at that," the Digger said, "a hundred and sixty-five thousand a year and the bastard can't get the fuckin' ball outa the fuckin' outfield, for Christ sake."

"I assume you're not down on them," the Greek said.

72

"Line's wrong," the Digger said. "No way them bastards get five more'n Cleveland, McDowell there. I laid off."

"Still at it," the Greek said. "I'm beginning to see it, now, how it happened. You just haven't got no fuckin' *sense,* is all."

The Digger thought for a moment. "That's about right," he said, "I think that's about right. I start off, blackjack, twenty-one, they call it. I had eight hundred and twenty bucks and three days and I'm there the first night, I just couldn't wait."

"The fuck you doing playing blackjack?" the Greek said. "My little kid knows enough, don't play blackjack."

"Look," the Digger said, "my little kid too. My holy brother. Everybody knows that, got any fuckin' brains at all. But see, I see this old bastard, brown sportcoat. He's betting thousand-dollar bills. I never saw more'n two of them in my whole fuckin' life, and one of them was queer, a guy, stupid shit, wants to sell me a hundred of them. This guy, he's got the genuine and he's peeling them off like they're onna outside of something he's gonna eat, all right? So, I got to be all right, I see that. I pay a grand, the trip, the eight-twenty's somebody else's, I'm peeling fives, it's gonna last me a long time, I lose every goddamned hand. Which, of course, I'm not gonna do, I'm too fuckin' smart for that.

"I win some," the Digger said. "I lose some. The old coot drops twenty of them things that I see. Don't mean nothing to me. I'm thinking: you grab that son of a bitch in the alley, before he starts, you wouldn't have to work again for the rest of your fuckin' life. So, he's got this credit card. You been to Vegas, Greek?"

"Nah," the Greek said. "I went to fuckin' Havana before that fuckin' Commie took over, I lost my fuckin' shirt. Nothing like what you did. About five hundred. I said, 'I'm not doing that again.' Got hell from my wife, too. I don't go for that shit, making other guys rich with my money."

"Your wife," the Digger said. "My fuckin' wife, she knew about this she would fuckin' *kill* me. Anyway, the old bastard's got a credit card. Shows it, he can cash checks. He writes out the check and this sleepy-looking cocksucker okays it. The old bastard gets his own thousands back, he starts in again. Only now, of course, he's out the check. Now right fuckin' *there,* Greek, is when I should've quit, right onna fuckin' *spot.* But I don't.

"I think," the Digger said, "I think, I'm different, not like the old coot. I had about sixty of the house money. I had eight-eighty. Beautiful, I think, old bastard's using up all the bad luck. I'm gonna sit there and make hay. He sits there, calm as hell, nerves like he's got he oughta be robbing banks, all I gotta do is bet steady and fast and I make a bundle.

"See what I mean?" the Digger said. "Stupid. No more fives. Twenties. Some good cards, some bad cards, I win some and I lose some, they deal them fuckin' cards like they're coming out of a pistol, bang, bang, bang. Pretty soon I haven't got no money left.

"I was surprised," the Digger said. "I had eight-eighty when I start playing twenties. I wasn't playing that long. I win a few. Can't be. But there it is, they got the whole eight-eighty back and I, I'm out of money.

"Now," the Digger said, "I'm not like the old bastard. I haven't got no credit card. But, the tour there, special arrangement and all? I can sign a marker. You know about that, right? You being the guy that winds up with the markers."

"Sure," the Greek said. "But the idea is, we're after the guys, got businesses and all, afford it. Not guys like you."

"Yeah," the Digger said. "A phone call would've gone good, Greek. I didn't know that. Where I find Richie, kick the living fuckin' shit out of him a few times?"

"I knew he called you," the Greek said, "I would've called you."

"Tell you what," the Digger said, "call him now."

"Uh uh," the Greek said, "you owe the fuckin' money, Dig. Too late now. You signed the paper, you owe the dough. No other way."

"I did," the Digger said. "That night I sign five of what you got."

"That's when you should've quit," the Greek said.

"Yeah," the Digger said, "I should've quit when I get onna plane, me giving the Greek all that, plus the eight-twenty I give them that they give me. My wife, well, it, I lost almost six K and it's still early when I get up, and you got no idea, the shit I took, my wife, I told her, I'm spending a grand, go to Vegas. Boy, I got up from that table, almost six grand down, it's like they had one of them hook-ups, I could hear her and she don't even know it yet. She still don't know it.

"I went to bed that way," the Digger said. "All that stuff they give you, all the broads in Vegas? Well, I don't screw around much. But I had it in mind, you know, things go all right, maybe I try a little strange tail. Well, that night I'm not interested in no broads. I couldn't've got it up on a bet. I was fuckin' *sick,* is what I was.

"The next day I get up. I feel awful. The kid, his girl didn't get her period, two weeks late? I'm the same way. I'm not doin' *that* again, no sir. No more fuckin' cards. Breakfast and then I'm gonna have lunch and then I'm gonna have dinner, but no more cards for the Digger. This is the first day I'm there, I'm already onna ropes. I'm gonna be a good boy. And think about how I come up with five for being stupid.

"Now that place," the Digger said, "they got that place laid out pretty good. The pictures they give you, you got swimming, you got the golf, the horse-back riding, you can shoot pool and tennis, they got tennis, you want to sit around the pool they got broads with big tits to look at. Great. Except, it's over a hundred, we're there, all three days. I never rode a fuckin' horse in my *life,* and I don't want to. And besides, they got, they don't want you riding no horses, they got them casinos open day and night. You go down for fuckin' breakfast, people gambling. Gambling's what they got for you to do. That's all they got for you to do. Unless maybe you wanna go the library, down the airport, watch the planes er something.

"I'm not gambling," the Digger said. "I sit around the pool, I see a lot of dumpy old fat kikes with baggy tits, they got white and blue hair and their skin, you could make shoes out of it. All these guys look like King Farouk flappin' around in them rubber things they wear on the feet, and they're all smoking cigars. Now and then you see something go by, little short of seventy, the old bastards look at her and you know, hundred-dollar whore, made out of sheet metal, you fucked her and you'd cut it off on a rough edge.

"I took about all of that I could," the Digger said. "Then I go to the movies. I fly all the way across the country and I go the *movies*. I gotta stay out of trouble."

"How's the movie?" the Greek said.

"Shitty," the Digger said. "One of them James Bond things. They show half of it, I don't care about the rest. You can't believe it. It's all shit. But I stay. I don't stay, I can go down the street and watch them press pants or something. It's not as bad as the fuckin' pool and at least I'm not losing no money. Of course I'm not making no money, and making money, that is what I'm thinking about. Every single goddamned minute. That and how if I don't think of something, I'm gonna spend the rest of my life, probably, being married to a saw-mill.

"I go back the hotel," the Digger said. "I still haven't got anything in mind. I meet Mikey-mike, couple the other guys, we have dinner. Food isn't bad, that I give them. Okay, and we see a show, and a couple after-dinners, and we pay and I get the change in quarters. They're all going back and forth, one of them gets a hundred off the slots, grabbed it right after this jerk in a raincoat that dumped about five hundred into it, next guy plays roulette, buck a turn, drops two-fifty the night before, still in pretty good shape and all, six hundred buckos left and he likes gold, he's out all day and he feels pretty good. Tonight he gets it back. And Mikey-mike, shacked up all day, hundred and a half, one of the guys says to him, 'Lot of bread.' Mikey-mike says, 'No, not for what they do to you for that. It's dirt fuckin' cheap.'

"So I'm all," the Digger said, "I feel bad, you know? Everybody's having a good time, got sense enough, pace themselves, I hadda spend the day inna movies because I'm a big asshole. So I think, Shit, I

76

can't spend two more days like this, I'll be an old man, the time I go home. I'll play the slots. Man's got to do something.

"Eight fuckin' quarters," the Digger said, "two fuckin' dollars. You lose six, two bucks more, don't scare you much. I play nice and slow. Make them last. Them things're rigged there. Every so often you win a little something, keep you interested. Pretty soon, though, no more quarters. There's this woman there, got to be four hundred years old. Plays three machines all at once. I watch her. She talks, you know? Can't hear what she says, just talks all the time. I was lower'n I've ever been in my life. I get change a five. The Digger, I got nickels. I'm playin' fuckin' nickels.

"I lose and I lose," the Digger said. "The old lady leaves, probably going some place, have a nice quiet heart attack or something. I jackpot nickels. Beautiful. Why the fuck don't I jackpot quarters? Never mind, God don't hate me after all. I got, I got probably two hundred and fifty nickels. In paper cups. I take them over the change booth. 'Gimme quarters.'

"Two paper cups full of quarters," the Digger said. "I take one the old lady's machines. Might as well get it over with. Eight quarters. Ten quarters. Twenty quarters, it keeps on eating them. I haul the lever. Jackpot, quarters. Fifty bucks.

"I go the change booth again," the Digger said. "Half dollars. I'm halfway down the first roll. I jackpot the halfs and now I got, it's one of them machines, you can play three lines at once, I got three jackpots.

"Now," the Digger said, "anybody beats the machine, there's this red light, flashes, they make some noise about it. Gets the other dumb fucks hungrier. You hit one on the fifties on all three lines, they put you inna Hall of Fame. Take a Polaroid of me, two girls in cowboy suits. One of them says to me, couldn't hear it unless you happened to be standing next to her, 'You wanna get the best French inna desert?' I'm too smart for that. 'The money,' I say, 'gimme the money.' Twenty-five hundred in silver dollars."

"So you go back to the blackjack table," the Greek said.

"Not on your fuckin' *life*," the Digger said. "I said 'Folding money. Gimme paper. I can't carry this stuff around.' Well, they got a lot of trouble finding that. I say, 'Look, no shit, all right? I'm not putting it in the dollar slots, I gotta get a truck, take it home. Gimme hundreds. I'll take fifties, hundreds is what I want.' They piss and moan a lot, but they do it.

"I go back to the room," the Digger said. "I went to bed. I felt a hell of a lot better'n I felt when I got up from it inna morning, I can tell you that. I'm not even, but at least I got something to work with. Tomorrow I'm gonna get up and think some more, maybe I end up getting my ass outa the gears.

"I get up the next day," the Digger said. "I feel pretty good. I go out the pool and have breakfast, a little vodka and orange juice, I read the paper. All the time, I'm thinking. How do I get out of this? How'd I get into it? Doing something they know better'n I know. Playing cards. I didn't play cards, fifteen years. I was always getting my brains beat out, playing cards. I don't know cards, cards're not my game. I know sports. I make a buck, it's because I know sports, I'm betting against somebody else, maybe knows sports, don't know sports so good. Okay, sports action. Sports action is what I need.

"They also got sports action up the ass in Vegas," the Digger said. "I have another vodka and orange juice. Already I feel better, I didn't do anything yet. This one feels right. The fat ladies, I don't even see them any more. What I need is the newspaper, sports page.

"That particular day," the Digger said, "Oakland at Boston. Oakland, Vida Blue. Sox've got Siebert listed. You do any bookin', Greek?"

"Bookin's for jerks," the Greek said. "No."

"Lotta rich jerks around, then," the Digger said.

"Because there's a lot of guys like me around, collect their stuff," the Greek said. "Look closer the books, next time you see a rich one, is my advice. There's a few. Not many."

"Well, I go down there," the Digger said, "Santa

Anita Turf Club. No change inna pitchers. They got Oakland, six and a quarter.

"Now that don't sound bad, you just come up and look at it," the Digger said. "Blue's hotter'n hell. But Blue's pitching in the Fenway. I remember a southie, pitched there once or twice, done all right, but that's Mel Parnell and he don't play for Oakland. He's a little retired, the way I hear it. Also, anything hot as Blue's due to lose. And anyway, say what you want Siebert, he's smart and he can throw that thing, and by now he's been around the Fenway long enough, he don't throw up when he comes out and looks at the Wall. I think, Digger, you got something here, isn't anybody else knows about it. So, they don't take no credit, the books, I put the twenny-five down on the Sox. Guy hears me, kind of laughs and says, 'You guys from Boston, you're too loyal.' I think, nobody gets six offa Siebert inna Fenway, but I don't say anything.

"They're four, no, three, they're three hours behind us," the Digger said. "Games, the game's at night. Quarter of seven out there, starts seven-thirty here, over by quarter of ten. All I got to do is find something to do till supper. I'll play golf.

"My brother plays golf," the Digger said. "It starts snowing here, the first thing he thinks of, he's gonna go down to Florida, play golf. Watches golf on the television. In February he's down the Cape, playing golf. Comes down, goes down to Scituate there every summer, that golf thing they got down to where Curley used to live. Me, I can't get interested in golf. Golf sucks."

"It's too fuckin' slow," the Greek said. "It don't go fast enough. You can get more exercise eatin' a fuckin' sandwich, for Christ sake. You walk around and walk around and you wait for about two hundred other guys to walk around in front of you. Golf don't make no sense."

"Right," the Digger said, "so, it's just what I need. I ask the hotel, can I rent clubs. I get out onna course. I played thirty-six holes. It's over a hundred. I'm all alone. I hate what I'm doing and I'm lousy at it and there's all these fat bastards zooming around inna carts

79

and having a hell of a time, and I walk and I sweat and I walk and I sweat some more. I played nine. I had three beers. Nine more, I had a sandwich and a couple more beers. Then I play eighteen more. Front nine, four beers. I don't sweat at all, now. I don't piss. I'm drying up. Back nine, I had three more.

"Now," the Digger said, "I'm half drunk, full of beer. I go back the hotel, my head's all full of air or something. All that sun, too. So I stop in the bar, do something sensible: I have a few beers. I got to do something, I'm waiting for the fuckin' game, I'm too fuckin' nervous to eat. I don't want to take a shower, it's too much goddamned trouble, go up the room and go through it even if I do smell like a wet horse. Hell, I lose and I stink like shit anyway. I win, I'm a rose. Blow the shower. Have another beer. Six-thirty, I stroll around to the book, nice and casual. They go extra innings, I'm gonna have a baby or something. Results up: it's a final, I win. I am fuckin' goddamned *even*."

"Good old Sonny Siebert," the Greek said.

"*I* would've bought him a drink," the Digger said. "He'd've been there, I would've bought him a drink. So I take the dough, I go back the hotel, king of the fuckin' world, all right? Take a shower, have dinner, all that kind of stuff, and I'm gonna fuckin' *enjoy* it, you know? I see Mikey-mike and we go and we have dinner, and I really, I hadda great meal, 'So,' he says to me, 'what about tonight? You wanna get laid?' I say, 'Nope, not me. I'm gonna be a good boy.' Well, all right, Mikey-mike's gotta leave, he's got this appointment to get blown and that, and I say, 'Go ahead. I'll sit here a while and then I go watch the show.' See, by then I'm getting over all that beer I drink.

"Well," the Digger said, "they got this goddamned fairy, comes out and what's he gonna do? He's gonna sing. Not to me, he isn't gonna sing. I call the waiter over. 'I thought I was gonna see a show,' I say. 'What's this faggot doing? I thought there's naked women or something.' He says, 'Inna lounge. Revue's inna lounge, weeknights.'

"I go in the bar," the Digger said. "I get a Wild

Turkey and I sit down. Then I get another Wild Turkey. Then the show starts. Waiter steered me right: naked women. I start to think: Maybe Mikey-mike's right, I do wanna get laid after all. Then the top girl comes out. That's when I decide, I do wanna get laid. That broad, who was that broad with the big tits, got killed in the car accident?"

"I dunno," the Greek said.

"Mansfield," the Digger said.

"Jayne Mansfield," the Greek said.

"Yeah," the Digger said, "her. Remember the tits she had on her?"

"They were big," the Greek said. "I remember that."

"This girl had bigger tits'n Jayne Mansfield," the Digger said. "I couldn't fuckin' believe, I never saw anything like that in my life. There's this guy sitting next to me, I'm at the bar? I said to him, 'Look, I know I'm seeing that. I haven't gone nuts or anything. But that, that's two guys in a girl suit or something. There's nothing like that in the world.'

" 'That's Supertits,' he says. 'She's full of silicone. Had one of them Japanese jobs. Fifty inches.' I say, 'Them things oughta go twenny pounds apiece. That broad, she shouldn't be able to walk around.'

" 'They're just like rocks, too,' he says," the Digger said. " 'You ask nice, you can get some of that. I don't recommend it, but you can. Three hundred an hour, isn't worth it. It's like fuckin' onna goddamned ramp anyway, and she thinks, she lets you pull 'em, she earned her money. You can pull those, you can stretch bricks. I was you, I wouldn't do it. You want to get laid, go get a good ho and get laid.They'll give you a ride for the dough. Less dough, too.'

"I say, 'No, thanks,' " the Digger said. " 'Way things've been going for me, I'd probably get cancer.' So he says, 'You been playing against the house. Everybody gets cleaned out, doing that. What you need is a nice friendly game.'

"Oh, he's got a great line of shit," the Digger said, "this and that, we get a group of guys together, he's up from LA with a group of guys from the barbershop, he runs a barbershop in LA, comes up to

81

Vegas because you meet a sophisticated kind of guy there, knows what he wants."

"You fuckin' dummy," the Greek said. "You oughta go to the Home, you shithead."

"I didn't go for it, Greek," the Digger said. "You can call me all the names you want, you got all the paper there, I still, I ain't lost my fuckin' marbles, you know. I know when I'm gettin' hustled. I don't walk out in front of trucks, somebody asks me to. I said, 'No.' So he says, well, he says, what am I gonna do? I'm going to bed. 'Good Christ, man,' he says, 'it's ten thirty. You come to Las Vegas, go to bed at ten thirty?' So I say, I told him, thirty-six holes of golf, all the excitement, I'm not as young as I used to be. Yup, I'm going to bed. So there I am. Quarter of eleven, I'm inna rack. Haven't been to bed so early since I was ten. I was fuckin' exhausted."

The Digger sighed. "One o'clock inna morning. Right on the dot. I'm awake. I'm burning up. Big white blisters on my arms. I got a couple on my neck. My face is on fire. Scalp's on fire. Now I know why them guys're running around onna course in the carts under the awnings. I got a charley horse in my leg. Goes on and off. This tremendous pain in the left arm. I don't know what it's from. My stomach feels fuckin' awful. My head's still all full of air, only now I got this headache, I hadda headache like I never seen before. I stink. I stink so bad I can't stand the smell. Then all of a sudden, the pain in the arm, it's the heart attack. I did too much in one day. I'm havin' a fuckin' heart attack and I'm gonna die. Oh, *Jesus.*

"Then I let this tremendous fart. I could've blown myself outa bed, all that beer, and it stinks to high fuckin' heaven. I'm sicker'n I was before, it stinks so bad. I got to get up. I got to *throw* up.

"I go inna bathroom," the Digger said, "I heave and I heave and I heave. The roast beef I had for dinner, the sandwiches, things I didn't even eat, I heave. Then I throw up bile, dry-heave for probably about three days. My spine's coming up any minute.

"Finally I stop. Terrible taste in my mouth, I have a drink of water and I brush my teeth. The water's

82

a, it tastes good. I had three glasses. Makes me sick again. Back down, heave up alla water, dry-heave some more. That time I don't drink no water.

"I get up," the Digger said, "weaker'n a cat. I got to get some Coke or something. Sweating like I did a mile and six furlongs. I'll go out into the bedroom and give the air conditioning a shot at that terrible stink inna bathroom and get room service bring me about eight Cokes.

"The bedroom was worse," the Digger said. "While I'm sleeping I probably been farting in there for about two hours, and the air's way behind catching up. I got to get out of there, the air gets changed, or I'm gonna be sick again.

"I thought," the Digger said, "I thought I was gonna have to beat up the bartender to get a Coke off him with no booze. I had three of them, he keeps looking at me. 'Costs almost the same,' he says, 'sure you don't want a sticka rum in it?' I start to feel better, stomach's quieting down. All that sugar, I threw up everything I owned of course, sugar's the only thing keeping me alive.

"Stomach's working," the Digger said, "now, the head. I go out, find a drugstore. Beautiful night, cold, clear. The air, really feels good on the face, you know? Different from inside. Inside smells like old ladies. I find a drugstore. Two Alka-Seltzer. I'm starting to feel halfway human again. I'm gonna go back the hotel and go to bed.

"You got to go through the casino to go to bed," the Digger said. "You died in that place, they'd have to carry you out through the gambling. Nobody'd mind. They wouldn't even see you.

"I feel great," the Digger said. "Come off a bender like that, always feel great, the head's clear, nothing in the gut, besides, you feel good after you feel lousy, feeling good feels even better, right? You appreciate it. Anyway, now I don't want to go to bed. Room needs time to air out anyway. I'll play a little blackjack.

"That was a great fuckin' idea," the Digger said. "Right up there with Jack Kennedy goin' down to Dallas, see how things're going.

"I pull up a stool at the high-stakes," the Digger

said. "I pull out the roll which Sonny Siebert's nice enough to get for me. Girl starts dealing the cards. Barmaid comes along, would I like a drink. Sure. I get a very tall screwdriver. Playing along, ten bucks a hand, staying about even, girl keeps bringing screwdrivers, I keep drinking them, tipping her with chips, and I stay and I stay and I stay. This new dealer comes on. Nice set of boobs, nothing like the monsters inna bar, but she's about thirty, they're cranked up nice and high there, I can look at them as long as I play. I play. I tip the barmaid a few more chips. All of a sudden it's daylight. I had about eighty dollars' worth of screwdrivers if you count what I tip the broad for them, probably a pint and a half of vodka in me, no food, and I'm losing.

"Jesus Christ am I losing," the Digger said. "I'm in a panic. I go up to twenty, got to get it all back. Sox don't play before we leave, no way I can get it back off them. Girl with the nice boobs leaves and this other one comes on, got a mouth she got in a store, very mean mouth. Deals just as fast, and I can't *buy* a hand.

"I think it's about eight in the morning," the Digger said, "Mikey-mike comes in, been out getting laid, three hundred bucks and they kept him leaping around all night and he's *all* shot. Not as bad as me, though. Comes up, says, 'Digger, Jesus, you don't look so good. What happened, your face? You been up all night.'

"That finally makes me get up," the Digger said. "See, you want to talk to somebody, you gotta get up and leave the place, somebody else can lose his shirt. Mikey-mike says, 'You look down, Dig. You lose the five you win, right?' Yeah. 'I hope you didn't go around signing no more things, there.' I pull out the paper. 'How much, Dig?' I don't know. I can't even tell him. He stops right there, we're inna middle of the casino and all these dead people're playing the machines and stuff, inna corner somebody jackpots and the lights're flashing and everybody goes whoop, whoop, whoop, and he counts and I stand there. 'Thirteen, Dig, that include the five?' Uh uh."

"What the fuck'd you do?" the Greek said.

"Look," the Digger said, "I couldn't kill myself, all them cocksuckers around, they would't've paid no attention. Don't do me no good, eat the paper. All I got's copies. I'm sick and I'm drunk the second time in a day and I don't have nothing on my stomach, I just look at him. He says, 'Come on, Dig, time to go home.' I slept all morning and they got me up and load me on the plane and I slept on the plane and we get home, I go down to Mondo's there and I have breakfast and coffee and I come home, sleep about ten more hours, get up and I said to myself, 'All right, professional fuckin' dumb shit, you're inna jam. You been inna jam before, you got out. Let's see how we get out of this one.' "

"I'd be interested to hear what you come up with," the Greek said. "You got a little problem here. It isn't like, I don't understand and all, but still, Dig . . ."

"Whaddaya mean, I got a problem?" the Digger said. "This, this's Tuesday. Friday I got a problem. I got two days before I got a problem."

"Friday you got two weeks of problem," the Greek said. "I can't give you no special consideration, Dig, you know that, but, well, I'm not nailing you no vig for last week, today. Friday, Friday you owe for two."

"Uh uh," the Digger said, "you're late. That's your tough shit. I was right here Friday. Nobody come around, see me about no paper. You can't sit there, tell me, you don't come around, I'm supposed to send a check to somebody, I don't even know who's got the paper, is that it? None of that shit."

"Dig," the Greek said, "Friday you owed the money the hotel."

"Right," the Digger said. "Way things're going, this week too, most likely. But I didn't owe it to you last Friday, because if I did, you would've been around. I don't see the hotel here. They come around, I'll deal with them. You, no juice for last week."

"Dig," the Greek said, "fair, okay? You lost the money. You don't pay the money, you pay the vig. I got to pay the vig, you gotta pay the vig me. That's the way it is."

"Greek," the Digger said, "you're a nice guy, I like you and you always treated me all right. I don't, I don't blame you for nothing, all right?"

85

"I'm glad to hear you say that," the Greek said. "I always thought, I was saying . . ."

"But you're a fuckin' *liar*," the Digger said. "You being an old buddy and all, I don't like to say it, but it's God's honest truth. You're a fuckin' liar and that's all there is to it."

"Dig," the Greek said, "I hope we're not gonna have trouble here, all these years, account a simple matter of business."

"Me fuckin' too," the Digger said. "But you don't owe no vig the hotel, and I know it, because I checked up on it and I know. You don't owe no vig the hotel. There's just one thing you gotta do: you gotta front the money back. That's all. They stand you thirty-sixty-ninety, just like you went into Kennedy's and bought a fuckin' suit. There ain't no vig, the hotel. I checked it. So don't gimme no more of that shit."

"Yeah?" the Greek said. "And where the fuck I get the money, the hotel? You want to tell me that? I'll tell you. I get it, my business's where I get it. I gotta get vig on dough I don't collect, I gotta pay out. I don't care what anybody told you, I gotta pay outa my regular cash. Who told you?"

"This angel," the Digger said, "come to me in a fuckin' dream. The fuck do I care, problems you got in your business? I got problems, my business, too. I come around and tell you, no dough this week, I got business things? No. Guys forget, ring up the beer, drivers leave nineteen cases, charge twenny, I don't come bitching to you. The vig starts when the paper's onna deck. Not before. You got some kinda problem with the hotel, that's between you and them. Nothing to do with me."

"Dig," the Greek said, "right this minute, today, you owe me six hundred. Not Friday. Today. Friday, twelve. Six and eighteen today, twelve and eighteen Friday. Now, how you gonna pay, or am I gonna have a problem with you?"

"Six?" the Digger said. "More shit? What's this six?"

"I'm doing you a favor," the Greek said. "Six is low."

"You think I'm a fuckin' chump, Greek," the Digger said. "I dunno as I go for that. You think you're gonna whack me six on eighteen and I'm gonna sit still for a screwing like that, I'm just gonna fuckin' let you *do* it to me? You know who you're talking to? I'm gonna take your fuckin' *head* off and serve it on a fuckin' *platter* to my fuckin' *dog,* is what I'm gonna do, and I haven't even *got* a fuckin' dog. I'm gonna have to go out and *buy* one, and I will, too, Greek, you know me, you know."

"Digger," the Greek said.

"Digger fuckin' nothin'," the Digger said, "horsing around with me like that. You're gonna juice me over three points a week on eighteen? You know the fuckin' rate's about two over five hundred. You know that. Bloom gives me eighteen for four big ones, I called him. I'll get it off Bloom. Fuck you. You're throwing shit at me. You come in here looking for money, I'm willing to give you money, I didn't think you're trying to make a fool out of me. You, you're gonna have a mouthful of *teeth* pretty soon, and they're all gonna be *loose* in there. I thought I was crazy, blowing the eighteen. You're crazier'n I am, trying to shit me."

"This is no shit, Dig," the Greek said.

"You better change some things, then," the Digger said, "some of the way you're thinking. *Nobody* shits me and lives. Nobody shits the Digger."

"Friday," the Greek said, "I'm coming back here. Twelve big ones from you, and I see you the next one. Otherwise, eighteen, and six big ones."

"Greek," the Digger said, "Friday I'll be here. You get eighteen and six big ones. But there is no way inna fuckin' world you see twelve big ones Friday. No way inna fuckin' world."

"You're pushing me," the Greek said. "I run a business. You know that. The juice's six. It's the normal. You signed the fuckin' papers. You pay the fuckin' rate. Everybody gets treated the same."

"Everybody that don't, that don't know he's being shitted and can do something about it," the Digger said. "I know, see, that's the difference, and I can do something about it, too. Try me out, Greek. I'm not one of your dumb shits, and you think I am, you think I changed, this oughta be fun after all,"

"I'm not gonna fuckin' *argue* with you," the Greek said. "Friday I come in for the twelve. You haven't got the fuckin' eighteen and I know it. Maybe then you'll be ready, talk sense, I got some work I could put your way. Maybe we can straighten this thing out."

"I'll be here," the Digger said. "Come in. I think now I'm looking forward to it."

8

"MARTY, LOOK," the Digger said. He sat in the Saratoga Club, members only. It was a long, narrow room on the second floor of a three-story building near the North Station. It was open at three twenty-five A.M.

Marty Jay had heavy jowls and fat cheeks; his eyes were large, almost bulging. He had very little hair. From time to time he wiped his skull with a maroon silk handkerchief, and the hairs stood up in swirls.

"I seen the Greek today," the Digger said. "Yesterday. I went to work, the Greek comes in. The Greek's got the paper."

"Huh," Jay said, "I figured Bloom for that operation. Looked to me like something Bloom'd be interested in doing."

"It was Bloom," the Digger said, "things'd be different. It ain't Bloom. It's the Greek."

"I wonder how come the Greek," Jay said. "Richie's got that. He's got some piano player in there, but it's Richie's. He never had no respect for the Greek. I wonder how come it's the Greek. I would've figured Bloom."

"It was Bloom," the Digger said, "I wouldn't be here."

"Maybe Bloom's sick," the fat man said. "Jesus, that's all we need, Bloom sick. That'd really fuck it."

"Bloom's not sick," the Digger said. "Bloom's around. He's not in it, is all."

89

"Huh," the fat man said. "Well, okay, Bloom's all right. What's the Greek want?"

"Six on eighteen," the Digger said.

"You're shittin' me," Jay said. "From you the Greek wants that? Infuckincredible."

"No shit," the Digger said.

"Oh for Christ sake," Jay said, "it's three a week, three points, and you cut it down. Five is right on eighteen. You, he oughta go you four. He's crazy."

"That's the Greek," the Digger said.

"Small shit," the fat man said. "Always was. I wonder why the fuck, Richie gets the Greek. I wouldn't touch the Greek with a pole if I was drownin'. You know something?"

"No," the Digger said.

"Things're all fucked up in this town with the shys, Mister Green dead and all."

"Mister Green's not dead," the Digger said. "You got a thing, you're dropping people off tonight."

"Mister Green's doing twenty down to Atlanta," Jay said. "If that ain't dead, it's close enough."

"Oh," the Digger said, "well, and that. I agree with you."

"Fuckin' guys," Jay said, "the only thing they want, get their name inna paper. Go charging around and they're doing this and they're doing that, ends up, you got the Greek doing things, he don't understand. Lemme tell you, Dig, somebody's gonna get hurt, result of this. Nobody gets hurt, Mister Green's running things, things're always quiet and nice. Now? Shit."

"Look," the Digger said, "I'm not payin' the Greek no six."

"I don't blame you," Jay said.

"Well," the Digger said, "I gotta do something. I got five. I need thirteen."

"Shit," Jay said, "see Bloom. Bloom'll use you all right. Bloom's fair."

"Yeah," the Digger said, "but then I gotta pay Bloom."

"What's Bloom want?" Jay said.

"Like you said," the Digger said, "four on eighteen. But I, I gotta wipe it up. I gotta get the thirteen,

90

I'm into Bloom, I take it, I either take eighteen and use the five for vig, I find something, else I gotta take thirteen and I use the five, I gotta find something, get dough for Bloom next week, you know?"

"Well," Jay said, "I mean, you owe the dough."

"Sure," the Digger said, "and I gotta get the dough. I got to do something."

"Don't make no waves, Dig," Jay said. "You start making waves, somebody's down to Atlanta. You, I thought you're retired. Better stay retired. Things're too hot. You're liable, somebody else's gonna go down Atlanta, you stir them bastards up."

"Marty," the Digger said, "I did something for Mickey."

"I *heard* that," Jay said. "I didn't believe it. 'Not the Digger, I say, 'Digger's retired.' You unretired?"

"I told you, Marty," the Digger said, "I need dough."

"What'd Mickey give you?" Jay said.

"Fifteen big ones," the Digger said.

"Not bad," Jay said. "That particular piece of work, I would've, I think three'd be about right, but hell, I hadda guy, take fifteen, I would've taken it myself. Good old Mickey. Guys like you buy him them Jags and the broads and all. Everybody's nice to Mickey."

"I didn't hear nothing from you, Marty," the Digger said.

"True," Jay said. "Of course you got to keep in mind, I didn't know you're inna market. That kinda stuff's sort of out of my line, too. Although, I hear what Mickey gets, I think, I thought about maybe going back into it."

"What'd Mickey get?" the Digger said.

"Hey," Jay said, "Mickey's in here this night, tells me, he's satisfied with the world, all right. Said you clouted him thirty checks, right?"

"Right," the Digger said.

"Construction company," the fat man said, nodding, "they use that account, payrolls. Also, credit rating. Ninety K in that account, every week, payrolls come in, put in what they think they're gonna need, runs about a hundred and thirty K. So, they

91

meet the payroll, and anybody calls up the bank, says, 'Am I gonna get paid, my rock wool?' The bank's gonna say, 'Sure, baby, you and everybody else inna world.' Only this week, the bank's wrong. The payroll's ninety thou heavier. That's Mickey's."

"Jesus," the Digger said, "that's beautiful. How's he know?"

"Broad inna bank," Jay said. "That guy, he must fuck them into blindness, things they do for him. Course, he don't screw you inna bed, at least, you done all right for him too. He's gonna run about five K, expenses, on ninety, he's Fat City and everybody else's full of shit. You included."

"Shit," the Digger said.

"Don't cost no more," Jay said, "go ahead if you like."

"Look," the Digger said, "you got anything?"

"I heard about something," Jay said. "First time, I turn it down. Too fuckin' risky. Nobody experienced to go along. Now I hear about it again. Don't sound so risky, I had some help."

"The fuck is it?" the Digger said.

"What the fuck," Jay said. "It'd take a guy and a guy, and a guy and a car, and they'd all have to be good guys."

"That's two plus us," the Digger said. "I can get the two."

"And a car," Jay said. "The rest of it, there's some other things, I can take care of them. A kid and some stuff."

"What's it worth?" the Digger said.

"You should've asked Mickey that," Jay said.

"I did," the Digger said. "I'm not talking to him now. I asked you: what's it worth?"

"All in all," Jay said, "I would say, a hundred and ten."

"Tell me how much for me," the Digger said.

"I ain't Mickey," Jay said.

"You're not Jesus Christ, either," the Digger said.

"I got trouble with the physical," Jay said. "The guy and the guy and the car, you pay them out of yours."

"Right," the Digger said.

92

"Down the middle," Jay said. "Just like always."

"Fifty-five," the Digger said.

"Plus the guy, and the guy with the car," Jay said.

"Must be pretty rough," the Digger said.

"Not for the right guys," Jay said. "Look, Mickey's stuff's smoother. You get hooked, straight B and E. This is tough. All kinds of people around. It's got some problems."

"Fifty-five," the Digger said.

"For the right guys," Jay said.

"I tell you what," the Digger said, "I'm gonna talk to a guy. I think I know another guy, got a car."

9

IN THE DOORWAY of the Regent office the Greek said, "Where the fuck is Y. A. Tittle?"

"Hey, Greek," Schabb said, "who?"

"Richie," the Greek said. He shut the door. "Richie's in Concord, I hadda guy, used to do some work for me, in Concord same time's Richie, Richie's onna football team. Quarterback. Tittle's the big hambone with the Gynts, then, they all start calling Richie Y. A. Tittle. Where the fuck is he, still in bed? Man oughta be able to be around by noon, good night's sleep, even if he does have a lot to do before he finally goes to sleep."

"Antigua," Schabb said. "Called me up last night, said he wouldn't be in, couple days er so. Lining up a deal down there."

"Broads," the Greek said. "Richie never lined up a deal in his life. He's down there getting laid."

"No," Schabb said, "guy called him, really looks good. We need it to compete. The other outfits, they got Curaçao and Caracas. Those're good items, you get the carriage trade with them, not just the hackers you get with Vegas and Freeport. Aruba, too. Richie's going to fly down there and look things over. KLM, they practically pay you to fly people into Aruba."

"Beautiful," the Greek said, "fuckin' beautiful. He'll fuck himself out down there. At my expense. I'm buying the bastard a third of ten pieces of ass and

94

a tan he'll use to get more ass up here. I'm losing my grip. I didn't use to be such an asshole."

"Look," Schabb said, "what difference it make? He said it'd be worth the ride to look into this. I agree with him. I don't care if he gets laid. Nothing wrong with getting laid. We didn't think it'd bother you."

"My friend," the Greek said, "I'm up here working for a living. I got problems, which I got from the last great idea you two guys had. He's down in the sun, goofing off, I'm paying for it. Who's tending to business, we don't all go to shit?"

"Look," Schabb said, "what's the problem?"

"The Digger," the Greek said, "just like I said. I was over there yesterday, that tony joint he runs for hard guys, he practically told me: go fuck myself."

"He won't pay?" Schabb said.

"He'll pay," the Greek said. "Said he's gonna pay, anyway. Gonna pay Friday."

"I still don't see," Schabb said. "I thought you figured, he wasn't gonna pay."

"He's not paying the vig, the first week," the Greek said. "He's not, he says he can get better'n the three points I hit him. He's gettin' it off of fuckin' Bloom, that fuckin' cocksucker. That shit Bloom, he cuts the fuckin' rate, I always knew he was a goddamned chiseler. And then some stupid shit put it out we don't have to pay juice, the hotel. I bet fuckin' Bloom did that too. So, I get screwed the first week, I get screwed the price on this week, it's getting out all over I'm high onna rate, and then the son of a bitch practically tells me: go fuck myself. I think he *did* tell me, go fuck myself. And you can bet, he's gonna mention that around town a few times, told the Greek to go fuck himself."

"So what?" Schabb said. "What the hell you care what he says? We're getting the money. That's what we're after."

"I got a regular business," the Greek said. "I got money out from here to Worcester. The way I do business, I make money having money out at good points. I get them points because people know, the Greek don't fuck around. Now, thanks to you and Richie and your goddamned fuckin' bright ideas, I

95

got this fat shit down to Dorchester running around, telling people I'm high, I scare, and go ahead, just tell the Greek, go fuck himself. That kind of thing, I came into this to get more business. I didn't come into this, get a lot of shit stuck on me, fuck up my old business. I was after easy dough."

"Well," Schabb said, "there's all that other stuff. You must be doing all right on that."

"I am," the Greek said. "The Jewish paper, fine, no sweat. Them guys go in for six points, they pay six points without a fuckin' whimper. I like doing business with them guys. How'd you get them?"

"When I was selling stock," Schabb said, "I had a little red book. It had good names to call, when I wanted to move a large lot fast. Interested, and the money was right there. Then, when I had a good deal or something I knew about, I would also call one or two of them. I want to tell you, Greek, I had one or two good dinners on calls like that. I like an appreciative client, boy."

"Dinners," the Greek said, "you must be an asshole, telling guys when to buy and then they make a mint and you get a dinner."

"Greek," Schabb said, "the way things are, its not when to buy. Any jerk can tell you when to buy: buy when it's low. It's when to sell. When it's not going higher. That's what I knew, and that's what I told them. Those dinners're in Paris, and there's six or seven of them, and they're all at Maxim's, get it? You check in at Pan Am, you don't pay for anything. The girl that's with you, your wife ever saw you, you'd be in serious trouble. On the way back she gets off in New York. You never see her again. You don't pay her anything, either. You go down to Miami Beach, you stay at the Doral and you play golf. You don't pay for that, either. When I went to dinner around here, I went in a Cad, and I didn't pay for the Cad any more'n I paid for the dinners. There're dinners, Greek, and then there're dinners. It all depends where the dinner is, hack it?"

"Oh," the Greek said.

"I didn't get in the shit because I was crooked," Schabb said. "I got in the shit because a guy that told me when the stuff was at the top, the guy that was making it go in the first place, got himself in the shit with the SEC. He was very tough, that guy. The minute they grabbed him he squawked like a chicken. I'm one of the guys he squawked about. They didn't even prosecute him, just us. Bastard."

"I was wondering," the Greek said.

"Look," Schabb said, "I was no more crooked'n anybody else. I was good and crooked. I just thought Mister Cool'd stay clear, and he didn't, and I guess I thought if he ever got caught, he'd keep his mouth shut, and he didn't. So, I took it right on the chin, and when I did I took that little red book with me. Those guys're reliable. They always pay. It's probably a good thing the bank examiners aren't around too soon after they pay, too soon anyway, because I've got just the slightest idea it's somebody else's money they're paying with. But you give one of them bastards a pen and a phone and the Market open, you'll always get your money, and right off. A month later he'll have that thing smoothed over so fine nobody'd ever be able to pick it up. You got honest money on that paper."

"Pure gold," the Greek said, "a hundred and eighteen thou, out in a week, two at the most, straight juice, a flat six K at least and we never loaned them guys a fuckin' *cent*. That is my idea, a tit."

"How about my other friends?" Schabb said. "How you doing with them?"

"The Protestants," the Greek said.

"Very few of them," Schabb said. "Some, maybe, but very few."

"All of them think they are," the Greek said. "Professional guys. Guy like that, starts in onna high living, he's generally good for about thirty-five K a year, got the house and the car and the son of a bitch, never buys a suit, it don't cost him two-fifty. There's a certain kind of guy, don't think he's made it 'less he's got on four hundred worth of knits and a twenny-dollar tie and he's getting his hair styled. Once they get that old razor cut, they think they know fuckin' everything. And boats, big onna boats."

"Those're the ones," Schabb said.

"Right," the Greek said. "I meet a little resistance, that kind of guy. He's got a house, okay, it's got a mortgage, he's been paying the mortgage awhile, he's run it down some, the house went up a lot. He don't have no dough he can get his hands on, but he's got the equity, you know?"

"Regular margin accounts," Schabb said, "that's where I got them. They call up and buy eight K, then they want the certificate fast. They're hocking it. Very little actual cash. Credit up the yin-yang."

"Sure," the Greek said, "I got a regular sideline in that kinda guy. Take the honey down to Puerto Rico, don't want the wife seeing no canceled checks. Okay, he's into me for a grand, he pays it back. They got it. The thing is, you gotta kinda pry it off them, gotta make him understand, he's gambling, okay, he got nothing for something. They're not used to that. Used to seeing something back for two or three K. New boat, goddamned station wagon, three weeks in Europe. Cards, he already seen the cards, dealer had twenty, he had nineteen, they don't want to remember that. Didn't happen. I gotta convince them it did. Takes time. Gotta call at the office, frighten the little honey, call the house, scare the wife, you heard me onna phone, you'd think I had something wrong with the throat. 'Where is he? I call him the office, he ain't there. I call him the house, he ain't there. He lives inna garage, that it? I understood he's a respectable citizen, owes me some money. Better have him call me.' They always call. Sooner or later, they call. They get used to the idea, they gotta pay. They go out, first they talk the wife down, Christ sake, I'm gonna kill them. Then they hock the Mastercharge and the stock and the insurance and they meet me and they pay off the whole nut. Them guys don't haggle. They pay the rate. Just takes a little time, get them used to it. I'm doing all right with them."

"So," Schabb said, "how much we make off my friends?"

"Four-four out," the Greek said, "five points a man, out by Labor Day. Eight, nine K."

"And you're still bitching," Schabb said. "We're making out all over the place and you're bitching.

There's things about you, Greek, I'm never going to understand."

"Mister Schabb," the Greek said, "that wraps it all up. Lemme ask you a personal favor, all right? You just tell Richie that, okay? You just said the whole of it, right fuckin' there."

10

"HARRINGTON," the Digger said, "how you doin' on that boat of yours, you getting anywhere?"

"Look," Harrington said, "everybody else inna world, it's Friday night, they haven't gotta go to work tomorrow. I got to go to work tomorrow, no Saturday for Harrington. You know why that is? Because I gotta, that's why. Just leave me alone, all right, Dig? Lemme have a couple beers just like it was Friday night for me, too. No guy that's gotta work six days a week to make the payments on what he's got is gonna see a boat he hasn't got already. I wished to God I never sold the boat I used to have."

"I know something you could do, 'd get you the down payment onna boat," the Digger said.

"Yeah?" Harrington said. "And then what about them others, I gotta stop going down to Saint Hilary's for my laughs every Sunday, hear what the Portugee's got to say this week about them poor unfortunate thieving Puerto Ricans that haven't got no money, I can work Sundays too."

"Well," the Digger said, "you played your cards right, might not be all that many of them, you know? You oughta be able to get a pretty good boat for thirty-five hundred or so, you could pay for more'n half of it right off."

"Oh oh," Harrington said. "Excuse me, I think I'm gonna have to go home right about now. I gotta go to work tomorrow, you know. I'll see you the first of the week, probably. I'll come in for a beer, we can talk about how the Sox do Sunday."

"The fuck's the matter with you?" the Digger said.

"Look," Harrington said, "I got a nervous stomach. I come in here a few days ago, your problem is, you're inna hole eighteen and juice. Now you're giving me, you're saying you got a way, *I* can get about, what, two grand, I do something you got in mind. You're talking about somebody else's money, I think."

"How much you make inna week?" the Digger said.

"None of your fuckin' business," Harrington said.

"Not enough for a boat, though," the Digger said.

"Not enough for a wife and three kids and a car and a house in Saint Hilary's," Harrington said. "Not enough for no lawyer, either, and it's a lot more'n I'd get making license plates inna can, too."

"Never mind the can," the Digger said.

"Right," Harrington said, "and don't do nothing that's gonna get you put into it, either, that's what I say. Lemme have another beer."

The Digger returned with Harrington's beer. "You can make two thousand dollars for less'n three hours' work," the Digger said. "You're sure you wanna turn that down, okay, I can get somebody else. I'm tryin' to do you a favor. You like working six days, you don't want no boat, okay, be a shit if you want, all your life. Just thought I'd give you the chance. Two grand for three hours."

"That's more'n I make at the Edison," Harrington said. He drank some beer. "The trouble is, the Edison never told me, go out and kill somebody important, and I never had the cops looking for me, anything I did at the Edison. Which is probably why it don't pay as good."

"Nobody's gonna get hurt," the Digger said. "Nothing like that."

"Dig," Harrington said, "my kind of luck, well, I didn't go to Vegas, you know? Because I know what'll happen to me, I got to Vegas. Same thing happened to you, only worse. I see the guys, I hear them talking, I know, they're doing some things. Okay, and they got more dough'n I have, and they get away with it, too.

101

But I, I wouldn't. Something'd happen. I'd get caught."

"You get caught driving your own car," the Digger said, "they don't generally hit a man too hard for that."

"Sure," Harrington said. "Of course while I'm driving it, the motor's running and I'm outside a bank and you guys're inside holding it up, and all the driving I got to do is get it in gear and make it go like a bastard and hope I don't get shot. Like I said, I finish this beer, I'll go home and say the Rosary with Father Manton onna radio, I think. Got saved from the temptation, there."

"Look," the Digger said, "here's what I want: you drive the car a place and you pick up a guy. Then you go where he tells you and you pick up two more guys. Then you go and you leave us all off and you drive to another place, and we come there and you drive us home. That's all there is to it."

"For that I get two thousand dollars," Harrington said.

"Yup," the Digger said. "I want a guy I can trust, do what I tell him to do."

"And that little ride and all," Harrington said, "that's gonna get you out of this hole you're in now."

"Yeah," the Digger said.

"And nobody's gonna get shot," Harrington said, "and there isn't gonna be every cop in Boston looking up his ass all the time."

"Look," the Digger said, "the only way you could shoot a guy on this job is, you'd have to bring a guy along to shoot, is all. If I ever see a tit, Harrington, this here's a tit."

"What is it?" Harrington said.

"Uh uh," the Digger said, "that's not the way it goes. I make a rule, long time ago, I don't tell anybody what it is until after he decides, he's in or not. You in or not?"

"How can I, what do you think I'm gonna do?" Harrington said. "Say I'm gonna do something, I don't even know what it is I'm gonna do? I never done anything like this before. Take pity onna guy, Dig, tell me what I'm gonna do, I tell you I'm gonna do it."

"Look," the Digger said, "week from tonight, Labor Day weekend, right?"

"Yeah," Harrington said.

"Week from Sunday night, you're gonna pick me up and then you're gonna pick up two other guys, and you take us, about a twenny-minute drive," the Digger said. "This is before midnight. About two hours later, sometime around two in the morning, you pick up, you pick us up, and you drop us off. That's it."

"For that I get two thousand dollars," Harrington said.

"Yeah," the Digger said.

"Right off," Harrington said. "I finally get to bed Labor Day, I'm gonna have two thousand onna bureau I didn't have when I get up."

"No," the Digger said, "nobody's got the dough Monday. You'll have to wait a little bit."

"How long?" Harrington said.

"Look," the Digger said, "I dunno. It can take a little time to get the dough, one of these things. Inside a week or so, I guess. But I personally guarantee you, you get the dough."

"Yeah," Harrington said, "but maybe something happens to you. I still get the dough? I mean, where's that leave me?"

"Better off'n I am, something's gonna happen to me," the Digger said. "Look, I get hit by a truck, you haven't got your dough, you do the best you can. You might get fucked."

"That's what I thought," Harrington said.

"Look," the Digger said, "you had two thousand in the bank, any time you wanted that dough you could go down the bank and take it out, and it's, you got a guarantee, right? That's why this thing, you're listening to me because you don't have it in the bank, you did and you'd be down to Green Harbor with all the rest of the fat bastards. They, the money that's here is here for somebody that hasn't got it and wants it."

"I don't know," Harrington said.

"Okay," the Digger said, "that's fine. I'm gonna take that, you're not interested. And one more thing: forget you had this talk with me, right? I wouldn't

103

want to think you went out and told somebody anything."

"I didn't mean that," Harrington said.

"You're a nice guy," the Digger said, "I like you. But you either gotta shit or get offa the fuckin' pot, is all, I haven't got time to wait around while you go this way and that and say, 'Gee, Digger, gee.' I like things to go right when I do something, get everything all set up ahead of time so everybody knows what he's gotta do and what the other guys've gotta do. So make up your fuckin' mind."

"I wished I knew more about it," Harrington said.

"You know all you're gonna know unless you come in," the Digger said. "I told you as much as I'm gonna."

Harrington said he would have another beer. When the Digger brought it, Harrington said, "Look, this's gotta be something pretty big we're after, two thousand for cab fare. There's how many of us?"

"Probably four," the Digger said.

"Okay," Harrington said, "four. I got probably the easiest thing to do, I'm getting the two, you said, you told me, it's gonna get you clear on the eighteen. Now I figure, that's twenny thousand dollars, and them other guys, they're not working for nothing. So there's gotta be quite a bit of money coming out of this."

"Harrington," the Digger said, "the two is tops. Don't gimme none of that shit. I can get five guys in ten minutes, do it for a grand. I'm being nice to you, get it? You want to stall around with somebody, go down the Lincoln-Mercury and pretend you can afford the Mark there. I don't go no higher."

"No," Harrington said, "I didn't mean that. It's just, this isn't no bank or anything, is it?"

"No bank," the Digger said.

"Okay," Harrington said. "Okay. No bank, I'm in."

"Beautiful," the Digger said. "I guarantee you, you'll never regret it."

"Now," Harrington said, finishing his beer, "tell me if I'm wrong. It's jewelry, right? Gotta be jewelry. Isn't anything else worth that kind of money, except money, four guys can move that fast."

"You object to jewelry?" the Digger said.

"Digger," Harrington said, "I object to no money, that's what I object to."

"You don't object to jewelry," the Digger said.

"I'd take pennies if I could get enough of them," Harrington said.

"Because this is something like your cherry," the Digger said. "Once it's gone, you're in. No way of going back."

"I know," Harrington said. "Where's the jewelry?"

"Isn't jewelry," the Digger said. "Look, you read the paper, what kinda ads you see inna paper this time of year?"

"I don't read them," Harrington said. "I'm always giving the wife a whole bunch of money for stuff, kids're going back to school and that, we gotta practically buy out Zayre's. I dunno. We're not stealing kids' clothes."

"No," the Digger said. "See, you're wasting your money on the paper. You oughta look at them ads better. We're stealing furs."

"Hey," Harrington said.

"Sure," the Digger said. "All them guys down the beach, they all think: this is the year I get the wife a mink stole. Them other guys, can afford the minks, their wives already got a stole, wear to the supermarket or something. They want nice chinchilla. So naturally, all them guys, sell furs, got the ads in. All over the place there's them trucks coming in with furs. And that is the real stuff, you know? That stuff moves."

"Holy shit," Harrington said.

"We're gonna get ourselves a trailer load of that stuff," the Digger said. "A whole fuckin' trailer load."

"We got a buyer?" Harrington said.

"This friend of mine," the Digger said, "he's got a buyer. Except, well, we're not really stealing furs. Look, the guy that's buying the furs?"

"Yeah," Harrington said.

"Well," the Digger said, "the less you know, the better off you are, but he's also the guy, you go back far enough and you look at everything and all, that we're stealing the furs from. He knows we're stealing them."

105

"Ah," Harrington said, "insurance."

"Yeah," the Digger said. "See what I mean, this's a tit? We're stealing insurance. See what I mean, safe?"

"Beautiful," Harrington said.

"You bet," the Digger said. "We take them furs out of the place that the guy owns, and we turn them over to a guy runs another place, and the guy that owns the other place is gonna sell them and the first guy howls like a bastard, all his furs're gone. Then he's gonna get the insurance, and he keeps his stock up, he's gonna buy from the guy we sell to. He's gonna buy his own stuff from the guy we sold it to, with the insurance money. Nice, huh?"

"Jesus," Harrington said, "I'd rather know him'n you. He's doing better'n any of us."

"No," the Digger said, "he don't want to do this, you know. He's gotta."

"Shit," Harrington said.

"You see the Super Bowl," the Digger said.

"Yeah," Harrington said. "Shitty game, I thought. Baltimore."

"Onna field goal," the Digger said. "Last-minute fuckin' field goal, all right?

"The guy that owns the stuff," the Digger said, "he missed the spread on that field goal. Cost him one hundred thousand dollars. He's been paying juice a long time. He's through. He's getting even."

11

"THE GREEK WAS IN," Schabb said. "He had a whole lot of things on his mind."

"I know, I know," Torrey said. "I got home, one this morning. I was absolutely *beat*. I actually, onna way up there's this girl, little heavy, but I look her over and she didn't mind, you know? I would've invited her up for a drink. Not this trip. I was so tired all I wanted to do was sleep."

"Well," Schabb said, "the Greek was right about that one, anyway. He *said* you'd fuck yourself out down there."

"The Greek, the Greek," Torrey said. "That don't make me tired. I been onna steady jump for almost a week. You see a guy and you talk to him. Then you see somebody else. Looks like a pretty good deal, but first you better check and see what this other guy can do. You're making calls, it's this and that, you got to fly all over the place on these dinky little planes that scare the living shit out of you. It comes right out of you. I, the screwing's not as good there as it is here."

"Keep that quiet," Schabb said. "I plan to say something else, it looks as though saying something else'd make a difference."

"Shit," Torrey said, "tell them there's an ocean full of mermaids down there, you want. They'll have a better time gettin' screwed'n I had setting up the screwing no matter what you tell them. Then I get

107

home, I take a couple aspirin, practically fall on my face I'm so drunk, I drink like a bastard onna plane, only way I can stop myself from jumping out, and then bang, six thirty, the phone rings. It's the Greek. That fuckin' guy, he was probably in bed before it's dark last night."

"He didn't go for the trip," Schabb said. "That was one thing that bothered him."

"I know," Torrey said. "And the Digger paid him out and pissed on his shoe for him, and now it's this and that, that fuckin' guy. That fuckin' guy. He's turnin' into a regular fuckin' pain in the *ass*."

"What the hell's the matter with him?" Schabb said. "He was all right when he started. Now, nothing you do suits him."

"He's got two things the matter with him," Torrey said. "He lost his nerve. That's the first thing. Then he gets greedy. All at once. He diddles along for twenny years with this pissy-ass little operation of his. Then he gets this. He starts counting his dough from this, and he likes that all right, but he's still sweating the diddly-shit he gets from the other."

"That's his regular business," Schabb said.

"His regular business is dogshit," Torrey said. "He's down the G.E. all the time, two hundred guys, five bucks apiece, six back on payday. The really big stickers go for twenty, twenty-four back. Chickenshit six for five, week after fuckin' week. He's had about three K a week turning over there ever since the Korean War, and he takes out six big ones a week. He don't pay more'n a point a week back, he'd had it so long, two at the most, he's probably got his own dough in it now. Fifteen, sixteen, twenty, thirty a year he takes in, and he's loving it. He should've stayed at it. Nobody ever would've bothered him. He was small shit and he was happy being small shit. He could've joined the fuckin' Chamber of Commerce.

"Then the fuckin' Strike Force gets Mister Green," Torrey said. "I still say it's a bad rap, conspiracy to, for gambling. Shit. Mister Green never touched no gambling in his life. Strictly money. He wouldn't know a horse from a fuckin' *beagle*, for Christ sake. He looked like a fuckin' minister or something. That guy was *big*. He probably had, I would say he probably had two or three million moving around."

"Cash?" Schabb said.

"Cash," Torrey said. "Checks made out to cash he gets back from the heavy trade, two mill at least. I bet I'm low. He was thinking about taking this, his case's on appeal and he decides its probably not worth the risk. But he wasn't very hot for it anyway. Too small for Mister Green, this thing."

"We can generate five thousand dollars a week in points on this," Schabb said.

"He figured that," Torrey said. "Matter of fact, he thought it might go ten, even more. 'But it's spread all over the place,' he says. 'I got to have guys running around. And this thing I've got, it could be problems. I tell you, lemme think about it. I'll give it to somebody for a while, this thing gets settled. I trip over something, I could get five or six years for this. I gotta be careful.'

"Yeah," Torrey said, "well, they turn him down, appeal, and he's getting ready, do the five. Only, see, his lawyer didn't tell him something, so he don't know, he thinks all he needs is somebody mind the store maybe two or three years. So he cops out, he says he can't beat it if he tries it, there's no way around it, his great lawyer says, he'll just end up getting more time if he does. Only, they got this new thing, they can do before they try you, they got this, they say, 'Organized crime.' You know what that does?"

"No," Schabb said.

"No," Torrey said. "Mister Green didn't know either. Well, they get you on something with a five-year top, they can whack you *thirty fuckin' years.*"

"Ah," Schabb said.

"And they did it to him," Torrey said. "Thing comes up, one of them motherfuckin' micks up there, and they give him twenty years. His lawyer's standing there, big dumb grin on his face, the judge gives him the twenty. He says, right inna courtroom, 'Twenty years? I hear you right?' The clerk says, 'Twenty years, to be served.' Mister Green says, 'You fuckin' *asshole*'; see, he's talkin' to his lawyer. The judge gives him another six months for contempt, on and after. Then the lawyer sees the judge after, talks him out of the six months. But he's still doing twenty.

"So now," Torrey said, "now, they revoke bail on him, and he's gonna appeal again, incompetence of counsel, but he's going away while they think that one over, he don't have no time, make arrangements, nobody can see him except his family, which he don't tell nothing to, and his fuckin' dumb lawyer, that he's all through talking to, he can't do nothing. So the other guys get together, they take Jesse Bloom and the Greek and they just, they give Bloom the heavy stuff and they give the Greek me. 'Take care of things awhile. Just take care of things, we figure something out. Don't get no ideas, it's yours.'

"All of a sudden," Torrey said, "all these years, Greek and Bloom're big league. Bloom, I think he would've made it anyway. The Greek, no way. He's playing with more dough inna week, he's used to seeing inna month. It threw him, is all. He's got everybody all upset. He's treating major guys like they're into him for ten a week down the G.E. People're getting calls: 'The fuck is it with this guy, he's gonna piss his pants or something, somebody doesn't do something.' And they stall around. And the Greek, he decides he needs some muscle up the Beach, he sends up a couple guys and he don't set them straight, they beat up a wrong guy, doesn't owe the Greek money. And he happens to be a guy, he's not into anything but he knows who is, and he's a guy that as a result knows some guys to call. And he calls them. And they don't care what Mister Green says, and they don't care what nobody else says, it's either the Greek gets taken off that stuff or they hit him. So, he gets taken off, they take him off that and they give him something a baby couldn't fuck up.

"Mill," Torrey said, "you can't shine shit. This's what they give the Greek. They give him me. They give Bloom the heavy stuff, the way they see it, they give me the Greek. See what happens, you got a nice thing up to Lynn and you start thinking, you got your feet up onna desk someday and you think, 'This could be all right?' You get the word back, go ahead, expand, and then they tell you, you win the Greek.

110

"Oh no," Torrey said, "I tell them that. That's what's the reason, nothing's moving up there, the word's out the Greek's got the old business and he's fuckin' crazy. 'You gimme Bloom. Mister Green comes out, I'll have a nice thing going here, I got a good man, help me, Mister Green can leave Bloom this and Bloom won't bitch at all. Gimme Bloom.'

"Nothing doing," Torrey said. "They're not giving me Bloom. The Greek. You want this, all right. Greek's part of the price. Bloom's doing all right. You get the Greek onna track again.

"I go see the Greek," Torrey said. "I hadda lot of trouble doing *that,* even. I call him, I get his wife. She says, 'He's not here.' I say, 'Have him call me.' Then I wait. He don't call. Next day, I call him again. I get his wife. 'He's out, he's not here.' Okay. I tell her, 'Have him call me, willya? It's important.' I wait. He don't call.

"I know what he thinks," Torrey said. "He thinks, 'All them guys screaming and yelling, Richie's calling for the Office. Gonna take things away from me.' I know that. He's not calling me because he don't wanna hear that. He's calling other guys, though, he's got time enough for that, he gets them calls all right. He's telling them, how good he's doing, he wants them to call me off. *I* want them to call me off. They're all laughing at both of us.

"So, finally," Torrey said, 'one of them says, 'For Christ sake, Greek, willya leave me alone, call Richie, willya? He don't want anything you got. It's something else.'

"He calls me," Torrey said. "It's like I'm tryin', collect a bill off him. You know where he picks, I'm supposed to meet him? Onna plaza, front of City Hall, lunchtime.

"I say, 'Look, Greek, you look to me like a man that was worried about something.' He says, 'I got a lot of big money out. I gotta be careful.' Careful, he says. Sure, we're talking about business in front of the whole goddamned world, he's telling me about being careful, fuckin' asshole. I say, 'Greek, willya calm the fuck down? The Office, they gimme something, I'm supposed to see you about business. There's

111

no contract, all right? Nobody's gonna do anything, you.'

"After that I call them," Torrey said. "I told them, this guy's gonna have a fuckin' baby. He's hearing footsteps. He's not gonna work out. I got a good thing here. He's gonna ruin it. For Christ sake, gimme Bloom, put the Greek back on six for five. *Please*.

"'No,' they say," Torrey said. "The Greek's my responsibility. He's, I'm what they're doing, the Greek keep him quiet, Mister Green gets out. 'Mister Green's not getting out,' I tell them. 'He gets out, the Greek's gonna fuck things up so bad by then, Mister Green's gonna have to sell razor blades, for Christ sake. Gimme Bloom, for Christ sake.' No, I gotta keep the Greek, Mister Green's gonna get out, the Greek'll have this, everything's gonna be all right. I don't believe them, they don't believe me. No, I got the Greek."

"Well," Schabb said, "I don't know about them, but I believe you, Richie. That guy has gone haywire."

"Of course he has," Torrey said. "I said, 'Look, this'll make the Greek worse. It won't make him better, it'll make him worse. He'll get nervous and he'll do something else. I can't control the bastard, he's fuckin' crazy. There must be somebody else. Lemme have Bloom. I can't have Bloom, lemme have somebody else, don't shit his pants, he gets the big nut. Not this asshole.' They tell me, 'No.' I'm supposed to shape him up and quiet him down. Well of course there ain't no way to do that. I tell you, Mill, you come around, I was interested, I talk to you, I didn't know it's gonna turn out like this, that fuckin' old lady, I really didn't."

"Hey, look," Schabb said, "you never gave me any guarantee. I knew what I was getting into. Maybe there's some way, we can get the Greek straightened out so a human being can live with him for a while."

"My friend," Torrey said, "there's only one thing you can do with the Greek, make him fit to live with."

"Well," Schabb said, "let's hear about it. This has got the makings of a good thing. I know, I can tell. There's a market for what we can do. There's nobody else trying for it, the way we are. We play this right, we going to take them guys and then get repeat business. We know the guys, we know the places, we know where we can get the money. We've got to consider what we stand to lose here."

"I know that," Torrey said. "I been looking for a setup like this all my life. No question about it."

"Well, all right," Schabb said. "Now, what it is, the Greek. From what you say, the only way he's comfortable is to have a lot of small-timers on the string. They don't interest us. If there's a guy that wants to borrow five bucks for three days, and that's what the Greek's interested in, for God's sake, let the Greek have it and we'll work this. We can really get something going. If the Greek's out, he's out. No hard feelings on my part. This may be a little hard. From what you say, the Greek wants the tit. Okay, let him have it. Get him out of this. They ought to understand that. The possibilities this thing's got, it's stupid to have the Greek in."

"That's what I tell them," Torrey said. "That's exactly what I tell them. It's stupid."

"He could wreck it all," Schabb said. "Look, this's important to me, you know? We oughta have a receptionist. We can get a good kid, eighty-five a week, all right? No shorthand or anything, but what we need her for is to answer the phone. It makes a nice impression, when we're both out of the office. We can make this into a high-class operation."

"Sure," Torrey said.

"We should get some rugs in here," Schabb said. "A nice blue shag, sort of turquoise. The tile doesn't make it. Somebody wants a big tour lined up, you think I'll bring him up here? This looks like a boiler room. We need more space. We should knock the wall out and go through. We should have private offices. We should have about six drawers, six stacks of filing cabinets."

"What're we gonna put in them?" Torrey said.

"You stick around," Schabb said. "I met a girl the other night. Works down at the airport. For two bucks a copy she's going to get me a copy of every international passenger manifest that comes through her desk.

Name and address, every son of a bitch that's got the dough to fly out of the country."

"Some of them're on expense accounts," Torrey said.

"Because they're making big money," Schabb said. "That's why they're flying out of the country on expense accounts. That's what we put in the files."

"I'm not arguing with you," Torrey said.

"This could be a blockbuster operation," Schabb said. "I had half a chance here, I could be doing better'n I was doing before I got grabbed."

"Except for the Greek," Torrey said.

"That's the way I see it," Schabb said. "That's the way you tell it to me, and I don't have any reason to argue with you, either. I really need this, Richie. I'm used to having things better than I got them right now. I'd like to see this turn into something."

"And it's the Greek," Torrey said, "the fuckin' Greek that's fucking it up. He even pisses and moans about the rent."

"Richie," Schabb said, "we gotta do something about the Greek."

"Well," Torrey said, "there's only one thing you can do, like I said."

"Which is?" Schabb said.

"Lemme think awhile," Torrey said. "Lemme talk to some people, too."

12

ON THE SOUTHERLY SIDE of Hancock Street in the North End of Boston, between Saint Sebastian's Church and the Foreign Seafarers' Mission, there is a block of three-story weathered brick buildings. The windows of the block are very narrow, framed in white-painted wood, glazed and puttied every year.

On the first floor there is a butcher shop (specializing in veal cutlets and select cuts of pork), a drugstore (advertising Kodak film and Phillip's Milk of Magnesia), and a variety store (in pink neon lights: "late papers—espresso"). On the second floor there are several businesses: a small insurance company, acting as agent, the only agent, for its own policies; a loan company which does not advertise; and Thomasina's Restaurant. There is no sign outside for Thomasina's.

At seven twenty-five in the steamy twilight of the end of summer, Croce Torre in dark suit pants and a white shirt, open at the neck, stood on the sidewalk and listened to the children. Men in dark suit pants and white shirts, open at the neck, lounged against parked cars and discussed the difficulties encountered by the Conigliaros in major-league baseball. One leaned against a Buick and folded his arms. "The managements're all Irish. What's the manager, Polish? I dunno what Yawkey is. He's from the South someplace. How come it's Rico and Billy C, there, they got all the trouble? Yaz? He's Polish too. He can't do no wrong. You take Tony. Tony hits a lot of homers, there. They give him a contract the rest of his life, like Yaz, there? No. They trade him. His eyes're bad. Okay, how come he hits all them homers?"

Torre entered an unmarked door opening on a narrow flight of worn, wooden stairs. The light was one naked bulb. He climbed into the main dining area. There was no door. The light was dim white bulbs and brilliant blue bulbs. The room was festooned with plastic grapevines. On the tables there were Chianti bottles with the wax of dead candles stubbed in the necks. There was a broad brown fan suspended from the ceiling; it turned slowly in the murmur of talk from small groups of men, and young couples, seated at the tables.

Thomasina stood ten feet from the top of the stairs. She was five-six and a hundred and sixty-six pounds. She wore a black beaded dress. Torre nodded to her. She nodded in return, angling her nod to her right.

Torre parted the beaded curtain to the internal corridor and stepped through. On his left the corridor was open to the kitchen. Three men handled stainless-steel pots in extreme heat under bright lights in the heavy smell of tomatoes and oil. In the far corner a youth pounded veal with the flat of a wooden-handled cleaver. At the end of the corridor there was a paneled door.

Torre opened the door to the private dining room. He was hit with cold air from an oversized window air conditioner.

In the room there were several Formica-topped tables pushed up against the walls. Upside down, on top of the tables, were bentwood chairs with rush seats. In the center of the room there was one rectangular table. Four chairs had been placed around it. The chair nearest the door was vacant.

Torre shut the door. He bowed very slightly. He said, "Thank you for coming." He sat in the vacant chair.

On his left sat Giuseppe Maglia. He was seventy-six years old. He had lost most of his hair. He wore a black suit with narrow lapels, and a pale-blue Oxford-cloth shirt. It was open at the throat. His nose was sharp and long. His eyebrows were white and bushy. His lips were thin and his eyes were deep brown and dead. He had a small glass of Cinzano before him. He raised it when Torre spoke.

Opposite Torre was Guido Masseria. He was forty-three years old. He wore grey slacks and a pale-yellow sports shirt, open at the neck. He had started to cultivate a mustache. His hair was black and razor-cut. "Our pleasure," he said.

Salvatore Barca sat at Torre's right. He was twenty-seven years old. His hair was blond, and styled. His eyes were blue. He wore a red polo shirt and a light-weight, blue, double-breasted blazer. His elbows rested on the red-and-white-checked tablecloth. His hands dangled below the edge of the table. In front of him there was a double scotch-on-the-rocks. He said nothing.

A young girl with heavy breasts, constricted in a white nylon uniform, entered from the kitchen. She carried a tray with four antipastos. She set one before each man.

They began at once to eat. They ate salami and artichoke hearts and anchovy filets and black olives, removing the pits from their mouths and placing them at the edges of their plates.

The girl brought a bottle of Asti Spumante and poured each of them a tumblerful. They drank.

The girl removed the antipasto plates and brought scampi. She filled the tumblers and took the empty bottle away. Maglia squeezed lemon on his shrimp.

The girl removed the scampi dishes and served egg-plant parmigiana. She brought clean tumblers and a bottle of red Chianti. She set the bottle on the table and left. She returned with another bottle of Chianti. She opened both bottles. She poured from one of them into each tumbler.

Maglia tore bread and used a chunk to wipe sauce from his plate.

The girl removed the eggplant casseroles. She served bracciole stuffed with pepper and mushrooms. She brought four dishes of zucchini.

Maglia said, "More bread and butter."

The girl brought a basket of bread and a dish of

117

butter. She refilled each of the tumblers and took the empty Chianti bottle away.

The girl removed the plates and the zucchini dishes. She served espresso and ponies of Metaxa. She said, softly, "Would you like dessert?"

Maglia stared at her. Barca did not look up. Torre said nothing. Masseria said, "Leave us alone."

The girl left the room and closed the door quietly behind her.

"Begin," Masseria said.

"It was an excellent meal," Maglia said.

"Thank you," Torre said.

"Begin," Masseria said.

"The trouble with the Greek continues," Torre said. "No matter what I do, it continues. He will not listen to reason. I cannot control him."

"You were supposed to control him," Maglia said.

"Don," Torre said, "that was because no one else had controlled him. He is uncontrollable. From the beginning of the enterprise I have constantly said that the Greek was uncontrollable. In the end he will ruin the business."

"He does not understand the ways," Maglia said.

"He's an uncontrollable son of a bitch," Masseria said. "I appreciate your problem, Croce."

"Have you tried to make him understand, Croce?" Maglia said.

"I've done everything I could, Don," Torre said. "It cannot be done."

"That's exactly what I mean," Masseria said. "He's an uncontrollable son of a bitch. Nobody's been able to make that bastard listen to reason."

"And it is what I mean, also," Maglia said. "All of this trouble that we have, we are relying upon people who do not understand the way that things are done."

"We haven't got no fuckin' choice, Don," Masseria said. "I been saying that all along. It's either people that don't understand, or nobody. Guys that understand're inna can. Mister Green went off, we had the Greek. He was the best available."

"It is necessary," Maglia said. "Very well. It is necessary. But because it is necessary, Croce, what have you done, to make him understand?"

"Everything except hit him with a shovel, I imagine," Masseria said.

"Croce," Maglia said.

"Don," Torre said, "I have argued with him. I have tried to reason with him. I have even threatened him. He will not listen."

"There is nothing," Masseria said, "nothin' inna world dumber'n a dumb Greek."

"He does not change, Croce," Maglia said.

"He does not," Torre said. "He can't understand the potential of this business. He will ruin it, if he continues. He worries about petty things. He is, he's a small-timer, and that's all he ever will be. I said so from the start. I wanted Bloom."

"You should've had Bloom," Masseria said.

"The enterprise," Maglia said, "can you run the enterprise without the Greek?"

"Of course he can run the enterprise without the Greek," Masseria said. "He needs a shy. Anybody can add, got muscles, can be a shy. Of course he can run the business without the Greek."

"Yes," Torre said.

"You know, of course," Maglia said, "the Man depends upon the Greek."

"The Man is badly advised," Torre said. "I said that when I was told that Mister Green had selected the Greek, for the Man. I said he should have trusted Bloom."

"You did not," Masseria said. "I remember that. You said they're both small-timers and you wouldn't want to have to trust either one of them."

"And then I said," Torre said, "and then I said, I hadda trust either one of them, it'd be Bloom. I didn't know how Bloom was gonna act then. Nobody did. But he was a lot better bet'n the Greek."

"Bloom did not understand the ways either," Maglia said.

"Of course he didn't," Masseria said. "None of the best of them ever did. Mister Green didn't understand the ways. You want a good shy, get a fuckin' kike. Never mind the fuckin' ways. Get the fuckin' money."

"I recommended the Greek," Maglia said softly.

119

"I didn't mean nothin'," Masseria said. "I was just saying."

"Don," Torre said, "you know of my respect for you."

"I do," Maglia said. "I knew your father. Your father was a fine man."

"My father knew you," Torre said. "On my mother's grave, I respect you."

"I know that," Maglia said.

"The Greek," Torre said. "I mean no disrespect to you, Don. The Greek will not listen. I cannot control him."

"Nobody can," Masseria said. "Whaddaya wanna do, Croce?"

"Bobby," Torre said. "I'm gonna have to knock him off. There's nothing else I can do. The fuckin' guy, that fuckin' guy's right out the fuckin' window, he's so fuckin' batty. Before he's through he's gonna fuck the operation. He won't pull out and he won't do what I say."

"That," Maglia said, "that is what you said when he was suggested, that he would complicate matters."

"I did," Torre said. "I said putting him in Mister Green's place was a bad mistake. I said it would end up, we'd lose a man that was perfectly all right on the small stuff, because he'd get a taste of the big stuff and it'd throw him and sooner or later you'd have to do something you wouldn't like doing. I said it, and now here we are."

"And I opposed you," Maglia said.

"I know," Torre said.

"I agreed with you, Croce," Masseria said.

"You did," Torre said.

"Barca supported you also," Maglia said. "I was the only one opposed."

"Mister Green would've sided with you if he'd been around," Torre said. "He was, he couldn't talk. You weren't unreasonable."

"Nevertheless," Maglia said, "nevertheless I was wrong. You were right. I will abide by your judgment. For me, you may do what you wish. To repair what resulted from my mistake."

"*Grazie,* Don," Torre said.

"You did this," Maglia said, "when you need not have done this. I remember that. You might have insisted, and done what you wished. I was opposed. You honored my wish. I was mistaken. You may do what is necessary to correct it."

"Richie," Barca said, "lemme ask you this: you really gotta knock him off? I mean, something else do it?"

"I don't think so, Sally," Torre said. "I wish to God I did, but I really don't. The guy's in great shape. He works out every day. Carries, too, he's got a fuckin' permit. Look, a thing like that, it'd take three men and a boy, move him around. The gun and all, I wouldn't want to be any one of them. It's either hit him or live with him. Nothin' inna middle."

"I'm sorry to hear that," Masseria said. "The Greek, who gives a goddamn about the Greek. But, I'd rather see somebody mark him up some."

"Me too, Bobby," Torre said. "The thing is, you just can't do it, is all. Look, I don't hate the guy, I had my way, I'd say to him: 'Greek, it didn't work. Go on back the G.E. and hustle the chickenshit. No hard feelings.' He'd knock my teeth down my throat. I gotta hit him and he knows I gotta hit him. It's either him er me."

"You want a contract?" Barca said.

"Nah, Sal," Torre said. "He knows it, but he don't really think I got the balls to do it. I can handle this one."

"Ah," Maglia said.

"Tell us what you want, Croce," Masseria said.

"Just the go-ahead," Torre said. "This interest of ours. I was interested in what you thought."

"Sure," Masseria said, "I go along. You can't do nothing else. There isn't a day goes by, somebody doesn't come bitching to me about the Greek. Do the best you can. Take him out. Do me a fuckin' favor. I won't hold it gainst you."

Torre looked at Barca. "Look, Richie," Barca said, "you're there. I'm not. I agree with Bobby. Sooner or later the guy's gonna have to be hit. He's not a bad guy. He's just a jerk. We made a mistake. Okay, we done that before. A beating won't do it, okay, forget

121

it, don't work him over. Hit him. The business, I think the thing's the business. Protect the business. You got something there you can build on."

"Don?" Torre said.

"Your father would be proud of you," Maglia said. "He also was a man."

"*Grazie,* Don," Torre said. "You will, you will tell the Don? You will see that he is told? And Mister Green?"

"For you, " Masseria said, "I'm the Don. The Don is told. Hit him clean."

Torre looked at Maglia. "He is the Don for you," Maglia said.

In the heat of the late evening the Oldsmobile Ninety-eight Classic Sedan pulled away with its windows rolled up tight, Masseria driving, Maglia riding. Torre and Barca watched the car leave. On Hancock Street the children had gone to bed. The men talked.

"And another thing," said the man who still leaned on the Buick, "they never treated Zarilla right, either."

In the group on the sidewalk a voice responded: "Jimmy, fuck off, willya?"

"You keep a straight face better'n any man I know," Barca said.

"Whaddaya mean?" Torrey said.

"How you can go through that shit, I dunno," Barca said. "I seen it and I seen it and now I see it again. You didn't order no fuckin' snails. How come?"

"I hate snails," Torrey said.

"So do I," Barca said. "But still, you done everything else, make believe we're still in Palermo or something."

"Look," Torrey said, "he's an old man. He knew my father. The thing is, it don't take much trouble keeping him happy. My father went back to Naples, the Don come around with the dough and the groceries, I was just a little kid. I'm not gonna forget that. A thirty-dollar dinner? I think it's a fuckin' bargain."

"Of course your old man," Barca said.

"Of course my old man hadda run, he hit somebody for the Don and the Don made him take the beef," Torrey said. "So what? I was nine, the old man screwed. I knew him pretty good. He was a mean bastard. We, we're better off, the Don's bringing the pork

122

chops around. The Don never beat me up. I was in Concord, there? My wife always had the rent paid. The Don did that. He never said nothing, I still know who did it. The wife's using the place to fuck other guys, of course, but he don't know that. His heart's inna right place, Sally. I'm just trying to be decent back, is all."

"It'll get you in trouble," Barca said.

"How, it'll get me in trouble?" Torrey said. "I do all right."

"Two ways," Barca said. "He was saying, 'fore you come up, he thinks you oughta get made."

"Uh uh," Torrey said, "hopping around with the goddamned paper burning in my hand. None of that shit."

"I did it," Barca said.

"You maybe had something to gain," Torrey said. "I don't. Sooner or later they catch up with some guy, got made the same time you did, he's gonna spill his guts as usual, like every other goddamned ghinny I hear about lately. Then you go to bed at night, you got a state cop under the window. In the morning you get up, FBI onna doorstep. The afternoon, you're having lunch, Treasury guys swap the FBI guys off. Internal Revenue in the dinnertime. Fuck that. My idea, getting made's a great idea, you want police protection. Otherwise, fuck it."

"Okay," Barca said, "keeping in mind you just fuck me out of a ten-K contract onna Greek, I dunno why I'm being so nice to you, but you better think up some way, talk the Don out of the christening, you know? He's gonna have the wind up his ass, after this. He'll be promoting you all over the place."

"Tell you what," Torrey said, "tell him I'm a degenerate."

"No shit," Barca said.

"So I'm told," Torrey said. "Greek says that."

"What is it?" Barca said. "Little boys and dogs and that stuff?"

"Oh for Christ sake," Torrey said. "No, girls. Always girls. I just do some things with them, is all."

"Oh, shit," Barca said. "I thought you meant there's something wrong with you, for Christ sake. You're gonna have to think up something better'n that. You're gonna be slitting chicken necks and drinking blood with him, before you're through."

"No," Torrey said, "no, I told you. I'm not doing it. I don't get no edge from it. No way."

"Look," Barca said, "you know, the other thing, it still leaves that, you know?"

"Which is?" Torrey said.

"The day's gonna come," Barca said, "it's not here already. We're gonna have to whack him out."

"Oh Christ," Torrey said, "he's an old man. He don't crowd anybody. He don't want anything."

"I still say," Barca said, "it'll come. The Greek? The Greek's his fault. He's too old."

"God takes care the old," Torrey said. "So what, he made a mistake. Leave the old bastard alone. I'll take care of the Greek."

"This's about the ninth mistake," Barca said. "We leave him alone, we're all gonna be inna can. We're gonna have to hit him, Richie. Sooner or later, we're gonna have to hit him."

"Sally," Torrey said, "you come up the wrong way. That's one way of doing things. There's other ways. Leave an old man alone."

"Sure," Barca said, "and hit a guy, never would've been any need to hit him, the old bastard'd listened to you inna first place. This kind of trouble we don't need, cherry tomatoes and a nice-ah-black-ah-suit."

"Lay off him," Torrey said. "He's an old man and he done the best he could."

"The best isn't good enough any more," Barca said, "his best. The Greeks we got working for us now, they oughta have something better'n his mistakes to go on. I was with you, Richie, right?"

Torrey nodded.

"I had it my way," Barca said, "the way I think, the Greek's the man with the claim. We took him in, he didn't work out, we knew he wouldn't. It's our fault. We oughta start acting like men."

13

"Look," the Digger said, "they got the trooper that the kid shoots onna Turnpike, right? They're all out with the dogs, chasing him through the woods, they think he's out in Hudson some place. This's the holiday weekend. Registry, cops, all of them, they're all out onna highway Friday night, they're all out tomorrow too."

"So?" Harrington said. "I could still get stopped, you know."

"Sure," the Digger said. "You could get stopped on Morrissery Boulevard, doing thirty miles an hour and minding your own fuckin' business. In a pig's ass, you could. Because it ain't likely, see, because there ain't no fuckin' cops around. See, it's cops, do the arresting. You just go ahead and drive, there, like I told you. I'll think about things."

"I wouldn't think," Harrington said, "the moon and all, you guys'd want to tackle something like this tonight." He took the car up the ramp at Columbia Circle.

"Mikey-mike'll be right here," the Digger said. "Pull up in front of the station there. Moon don't make no difference. Nothing back of this place but more places like it. Nobody sees us."

Magro came out of the subway station. He wore dark-grey chino pants and a tee-shirt, navy blue. He carried a parcel, wrapped in brown paper. It was three

125

feet long and ten inches wide and two inches thick. He crossed the street and opened the left rear door of Harrington's Ford Galaxie. He put the package on the seat and got in. "Hey Dig," he said. He patted Harrington on the shoulder. "How's the virgin?"

"The virgin's nervous," Harrington said.

"In about a minute, here," the Digger said, "the virgin's gonna shit his pants, is what I think. He should've been on some of the fucked-up stuff we been on, huh?"

Magro patted Harrington again. "You should've," he said. "You wanted to see nervous, this thing, this thing's a . . ."

"Tit," the Digger said.

"A tit," Magro said.

"Look," Harrington said, putting the car in gear, "we sit here long enough, talking about tits, we're gonna have half the cops in Boston writing down license numbers. Where're we supposed to go now?"

"Expressway north," the Digger said. "I'll tell you, when to get off."

"Look," Harrington said, "you can tell me now. I'm not gonna jump out."

"I could tell you if I could ever remember which one it is," the Digger said. "It's either the Logan ramp you take, the tunnel, or else it's the Garden one. I can never remember which one it is, it's one of them. I see it, I'll know."

"Nice night," Magro said.

"Harrington don't like the moon," the Digger said. "I was telling him: moon don't take no pictures."

"Shit, no," Magro said. "Moon's good, actually. Remember that night we go down the Sylvania, there, Dig? Hadda nice moon that night."

"Time we got the swerve from Maloney and them," the Digger said. "Sure, moon saved our ass that night."

"You could've read a newspaper," Magro said, "there's so much fuckin' moon that night. So it's me, Harrington, it's me and Dig and another guy . . ."

"Brennan," the Digger said.

"Yeah," Magro said, "Brennan, and shit, we dunno what we're doing. Go over to Arliss, get a truck, go down there like we're three fuckin' idiots out for a ride."

"And then we're supposed to pay somebody about half what we're gonna get from the whole job, just for the goddamned truck," the Digger said. "We didn't know fuckin' anything."

"Marchi," Magro said, "Teddy Marchi. Minute he looks at us he knows what dumb fucks we are."

"Yeah," the Digger said, "got himself shot, later on."

"Down to Wally's Grove," Magro said. "They had this big argument about a trailer truck, cops all over the place, guys running around, hiding behind trees and stuff, bullets all over and everything, old Teddy walked right into the middle of it. Ka-blam, end of Teddy."

"Teddy should've stuck to minding his own fuckin' business that night," the Digger said. "There was one or two guys around said it's Teddy's fault they had that trouble about the trailer truck inna first place. Teddy was too fuckin' cute for his own good a few times."

Magro tapped Harrington on the shoulder. "So we go over Neponset," he said, "North Quincy there, and we take a left and we hook a right, you know how you do, and it seems like we're never gonna get there before morning or something, and we're all practically pissing our pants. See, we never done anything that big. We're gonna get, it was tee-vees, wasn't it, Dig?"

"It was either the tee-vees or the record players anna radios," the Digger said. "One time it's tee-vees, that time we got the terminal out to Dedham there, and then the other time, I forget."

"So Brennan," Margo said, "he keeps saying, 'When're we gonna get there, when're we gonna get there. For Christ sake, for Christ sake, for Christ sake.'"

"Brennan's pussy-whipped," the Digger said. "Afraid his wife's gonna find out. Cops, Brennan don't care about cops. He was nineteen, him and a couple guys tried to break in the South Boston Savings one night, they didn't know what the fuck they're doing, set off the alarm. So all these cops come, and somebody, lived across the street, seen four guys jumping off the roof the bank when the cops get there. Cops count up the ones they got, they got three. The one they haven't got's Brennan. This is the office they got up on the

127

parkway, there. So they got all these lights and they're all walking around and hollering and everything, and they can't find Brennan. Then there's this one guy, gets sick of it, he goes over and he leans against this maple tree and he lights up a cigarette, and he just stands there, watching all them other bastards running around, and pretty soon Brennan falls out of the tree, right on him almost."

"Got nervous," Magro said. "Started thinking about holding on and not making no noise, first thing he does, he lets go."

"Yeah," the Digger said, "and then it *still* took about five of them to get him inna wagon. So he does, I guess, three and a half, and he comes out, and boy has the wife, he got married and she's got him right under the old thumb. Eight or nine years he puts up with it, it's enough to make you puke, and then he finds out, all this time he's been scared shitless of her, she's out screwing this guy she knows before they got married. Seems he come by and fix the stove, he working for the gas company, he fixes her too. Poor fuckin' bastard."

"I never knew Brennan, I guess." Harrington said.

"He's over to Walpole," Magro said. "Went in before you come around."

"Take it easy, Harrington," the Digger said. "Wasn't for nothing like this."

"No," Magro said, "it's for killing her. Beat her fuckin' head in with a paira pliers. I would've done the exact same thing. All the shit he took, and then find that out, I wouldn't care if there was ten cops waiting outside to grab me as soon's I finish and shoot me right there, I still would've done it."

"Nobody ever did no time for something like this," the Digger said. "It's impossible. All the jobs're like this, there wouldn't be nothing but guys like Brennan over to Walpole, that killed their wives er something."

Harrington's car emerged from the Central Artery underpass. Traffic was moderate. "Start getting over to the right, there," the Digger said. "I think, yeah, take the next one, that says Callahan Tunnel. Then, you come the bottom of the ramp, go up across there, by the fish market. See the fish market? And you get up there, you take the next left and go right around under there."

Harrington drove past Giuffre's Market and the Digger directed him into the Market area. On the right sidewalk of the empty street a man in a maroon polo shirt and grey slacks walked slowly toward Faneuil Hall. "That's him," the Digger said.

"Right on time," Jay said, as he opened the right rear door. "Right onna fuckin' button. That's all right."

"Hey, Marty," Magro said, "good to see you."

"Always a pleasure," Jay said, getting in. "Mikey-mike, right?"

"Right," Magro said, "been a long time."

"I been doing some other things," Jay said.

"Harrington," the Digger said, "this here's Harrington."

"Harrington," Jay said, patting him on the right shoulder. "Okay, I can see I'm gonna have to go down and get the rabbi to fix me up after tonight. This's like the Hibernians' picnic."

"Look," the Digger said, "you could talk your own guys into taking a chance now and then, you wouldn't have to."

"Hey," Jay said, "where the fuck you think we get this thing, it's not my guys."

"Where now?" Harrington said.

"Jumpy as hell, this one," the Digger said. "Cars all set?"

"They're not," Jay said, "I'll find that fuckin' kid and brain him. You know where Valle's is, Route Nine?"

"Yeah," Harrington said.

"Go there," Jay said. "Now, there's a turnoff right when you get past it, going towards Worcester. Forget about it. I want you to go all the way up past the next set of lights, and then turn and come back to it."

"How come?" Magro said.

"So it looks like we're coming from the ballgame out to the stadium, there. Last time they play, I'm out at Valle's with the wife and a whole bunch of guys come by, left their cars there and went to the game. So nobody pays any attention to them. Anybody sees us is gonna figure we went out to the game in Harrington's

129

car, stopped some place, had a few drinks and something to eat, horse around some before we pick up the other car.

"Same kind of thing at the other end," Jay said. "Guys we're meeting're gonna get there about half an hour before we do. They get dropped off, go in, sit down and have something to eat. In a while we show up, park the thing off to the side, get in the other car, there, and that's it. They get through, go outside, get in the thing and off they go, just like they left it there when they come in from Springfield. This's that diner right at Route Twenty, you know where I mean?"

"Lot of gas stations and stuff there?" Magro said.

"That's the one," Jay said. "You oughta get there about five or ten minutes before me and the Digger. Same thing. Go up a little ways, turn around, come back. There's an all-night station right across the street, you'll be able to see us when we come in."

"Candy," the Digger said. "My little kid could do this one. Pure fuckin' candy."

"I still don't like this moon," Harrington said.

"I was telling him, Marty," Magro said, "you remember the time Maloney sends Dig and me and Brennan down the Sylvania there? You're supposed to be buying then."

"Yeah," Jay said, "record players, wasn't it? That fuckin' Maloney. He tried to set me up at least once, I think. I couldn't be sure, you know? I would've had him whacked, I was."

"Well," Magro said, "that night Maloney's setting us up. Real bright moon, and we get down there, we're so excited we're practically throwing up, and there's guys in there ahead of us, cleaning out the goddamned semi we're after. And it's that fuckin' Maloney that's doing it, for Christ sake, give us the job in the first place."

"That cocksucker," the Digger said, "was I glad when he got it. Best thing that happened in a long time was they had the war down there onna the Avenue and it ends up, Terry's bleedin' to death onna sidewalk."

"At least he didn't know who shoots him," Jay said. "I give him that, anyway. I always thought he hadda lotta dog in him, but didn't none of it show that night."

"Bull*shit*," the Digger said. "He didn't *know* he was

bleedin' to death, you know. He was just being careful."

"Jeez, Dig," Magro said, "I dunno as you ought to talk like that."

"Whaddaya mean?" the Digger said.

"Well," Magro said, "I heard, it was probably you give him what he wasn't talking about that night."

"I heard it onna fuckin' radio," the Digger said. "I was nowhere near the place that night. I was up the place, I was working the Bright Red. Cut that shit."

"Yeah," Jay said, "I heard that, too. I heard something like that, Mikey-mike. And another thing I remember, about twenny minutes after Maloney died, the Digger's got all the stuff Maloney's supposed to've had. Of course he doesn't share it with anybody, but he had it."

"Now look," the Digger said.

"You did, Dig," Jay said, "you had all them shoes. Remember, you're trying to sell me shoes about two weeks after, I said to you, 'Where'd you get all the shoes, Dig? I didn't hear no shoes around except what Terry had.' And you, you never give me a straight answer, you remember that? There's only two guys in town that're really better off when Terry's hit. There's you, because it turns out you got all them shoes, and there's the Greek."

"The Greek had shoes?" the Digger said.

"Nah," Jay said, "Terry owed the Greek money. I seen the Greek after Terry's gone, and I said, 'Hey, Greek, see your customer there, you're always bitching about, got himself shot up a little. Hope you had the policy on him.' And he wouldn't talk to me, either. Greek ever get his money, Dig?"

"The Greek didn't get his money," the Digger said, "I wouldn't be going to Newton tonight, I can tell you that."

"And then there was that other thing," Magro said, "You remember that, Marty? There was an awful lot of bullets down the Avenue that night. The door Terry come out of, it's practically shot off the hinges. Now keep in mind, the Digger's got a machinegun."

"Ah, come on," Jay said, "you know better'n believe

131

that. That old fuckin' story. That's just a story guys like to tell, isn't that right, Digger?"

"Sure," the Digger said. "The fuck I'd be doing with a machinegun?"

"Well," Magro said, "you could've shot Terry Maloney with it. Them're all forty-five in him. They could've come out a grease-gun."

"Could've come out a forty-five, too," the Digger said. "I used to know a guy had one of them, too, kept it under the front seat of his car, last I heard, pointed it at a guy once or twice."

Magro and Jay spoke together. Jay said, "Ah, Dig, that was just in case of trouble or something, and besides, I didn't have anything against Terry. Except he tried to set me up." Magro said, "It wasn't my car and it wasn't my gun, Dig. Just a couple things I used to borrow now and then, when I needed something." The Digger, Magro and Jay laughed.

Harrington said, "You guys're making me nervous, you know."

The Digger patted Harrington on the right shoulder. "Nothing to be worried about, Harrington," he said, "Nobody's got anything tonight."

"Digger," Jay said, "you haven't really got a machinegun, have you?"

"Well," the Digger said, twisting around slightly to get his left elbow and forearm further onto the back of the front seat, "I, well, I'll tell ya the truth, Marty, yeah. I got ten machineguns, actually. You know how it is, you're inna booze business, you got three kinds of cops coming around all the time, you buy your license, you serving kids, you running the whorehouse, you keeping maybe some stuff in the cellar, nobody, somebody forgot to pay taxes, that kind of thing. They're always coming in and looking up my ass. I tell you guys something, I dunno why none of them eight or nine hundred guys ever finds my ten machineguns. Got them right out in plain sight in the cellar there. Big wooden box, got a sign painted on it: 'Don't anybody look in this box. Doherty's Ten Machineguns.' Beats me how come they don't find it."

"Couldn't've been the Digger," Jay said to Magro. "Digger says he don't even have a machinegun."

132

"Yeah, right," Magro said, "must've been that other guy I keep hearing about, got a forty-five auto with a fifty-shot clip, carries this telephone pole around with him, just nails her right up to the pole and lets off the whole thing with a wire. Must've been him. Or a whole lot of guys, all got forty-fives."

Harrington's car traveled through Kenmore Square. He took the left and drove up the hill past Fenway Park.

"Maloney was a funny guy," Jay said. "I never heard of him. Then all of a sudden it seems like there's nobody else around but Terry Maloney. Guys were saying you couldn't even start to think of something, five minutes later Terry's already doing it."

"Yeah," the Digger said, "and fuckin' it up. Every time the son of a bitch went out, somebody got shot. More cops down around the Avenue'n they got in the whole FBI. I bet I know six or seven guys, got in the shit doing something nice and quiet and the cops're so busy looking around for Maloney they see these guys, you know?"

"Well," Jay said, "there was Greggie Halb, there. Got grabbed down the track."

"Sure," the Digger said. "Terry set him up, though. The cops had Terry figured for what Greggie's doing, and they go and talk to Greggie, and Greggie lets them go right on thinking it's Terry. So Terry finds out and dumps Greggie. I didn't blame Terry for that one. That's about the only thing, though. Terry, he was a kid, he grew up out to Saint Agatha's, there, he didn't *understand* anything, you know? That was his problem. His family had some dough. His brother, Billy, the one that sells the cars, big asshole buddies with my brother, that's what Terry should've been. He didn't know how to do them other things."

"Billy Maloney knows how to do a few things," Jay said. "I know a guy, retired from the Post Office, wanted to be some kind of court officer."

"Oh, sure," the Digger said. "That kind of thing, him and my holy brother're down to five dinners a week, shaking hands and their pictures in the paper. But Billy, actually I think Billy's kind of a class guy. He give Terry the regular funeral there, just like he dies in his

133

mother's arms, what is it, that cemetery off of Brush Hill there, just like Terry's the greatest thing inna world.

"That was a funny thing," the Digger said, "none of the guys go, of course, because we all figure, what the hell, Terry's been tryin' to fuck everybody, all the time he was alive, he's dead, fuck him. But my holy brother goes, and then he comes down the place after and he gives me this big speech, all the grief Terry handed his family, Paul sure don't want me doing nothing like that to him. My great fuckin' brother. So I say, 'Look, I'm glad you told me. I was just going out tonight, see if I could get somebody to shoot me or something, looks like such a great thing and all. But seeing things, your point of view, I'm not gonna do it. I changed my mind.' So he got all pissed off and all. He always does that. I ever told him how Terry tried to set me up, he would've shit."

It was ten forty-five when Harrington turned the Galaxie off Route Nine inbound and entered the parking lot at Valle's. Jay edged forward in the back seat. "Supposed to be down in the back, there," he said. "Tan Merc."

"Keys're in it?" the Digger said.

"In it, and it's wiped down," Jay said. "That's a pretty good kid, you know? He's smart and he's dependable. You get him to do something, there's no complaints or anything and he does it fuckin' right. I'm gonna have to get him something bigger."

Harrington stopped the Galaxie behind the Mercury sedan. "All right," the Digger said, turning again toward the back seat, "you got the gloves, Mikey-mike."

Magro had torn the paper off his parcel. He opened the box and removed three wads of beige cotton. They stank of oil. He gave one to Jay and one to the Digger. He unrolled the remaining wad and spread out two thin cotton gloves.

"Jesus, Dig," Jay said, putting gloves on, "you must be getting old."

"I don't like it," the Digger said, stretching the gloves over his hands. The cuffs stopped an inch short of his wrists, leaving the heels of his palms uncovered. He

134

wiggled his fingers. "I just figure, this's big enough, look for prints. Might as well not take any chances."

Magro reached into the box and pulled out a heavy-duty bolt cutter.

"That's wiped?" the Digger said.

"Three-in-One Oil," Magro said.

"Okay," the Digger said. "Now, it's almost ten to eleven. Harrington, one thirty, you be waiting in the Howard Johnson's on One Twenty-eight next to the Turnpike."

"Gonna be closed," Harrington said. "What if the state cop come around, ask me, did my girlfriend forget to show up or something."

"Open tonight," the Digger said. "Coffee for drivers. Go in and sit down where you can see the lot. Soon's you see us get in the car, out you come and we go home."

"Okay," Harrington said.

"Now another thing," the Digger said. "You're gonna have some time on your hands. Take this paper and the box and get rid of it."

"Where the Christ I do that?" Harrington said.

"Well," the Digger said, "you look around some, is what you do. You asked me, I'd say, find a motel or something, shopping center, got one of them Dumpsters, and throw it in."

"Somebody'll see me," Harrington said.

"Oh for Christ sake," Magro said, "doesn't matter if they do. Nobody pays any attention to people throwing junk away."

"You didn't mention," Harrington said to the Digger, "I hadda throw anything away."

"Harrrington," the Digger said, "I also didn't mention you could have a couple cups of coffee while you're waiting for us. It's okay, believe me, you can still do it. And you're taking the garbage out, too, just like I say. So quit arguing with me and just fuckin' do it, all right? Just do it and be at the Johnson's, like I said, will you do that?"

"I'll be there," Harrington said.

14

MAGRO DROVE WEST on Beacon Street.

"It's a green Vega," Jay said, "right up here in front of the barbershop, 'cross the street from the Mobil."

"Where's the fuckin' U-Haul?" the Digger said.

"In the station with all the other U-Hauls," Jay said. "In the morning they had nine or ten of them, now they got ten or eleven of them, they stayed closed all day and in the middle of the afternoon, they're all home watching the ballgame, the kid pulls up, backs her in, unhooks and drives away. Calls me up: 'Went like a charm,' he said. 'Waited over in Cambridge, this dude comes along in a Vette with Michigan plates, I let him unload the trailer, he goes in the apartment the last time, I hooked it.' Then he tells me, he's laughing like hell, 'Tonight I'm going back and hook the Vette. I got a guy down in New York I call, gimme a full bill for it. Thanks for the job, Marty.' The Vega, I ask him, you get the car all right? He says, 'Grabbed her right off the lot in Brockton this morning. No sweat. Took her over through Randolph and took the plates off an Olds at the Holiday. Wait'll that guy gets up.' "

Magro stopped the Mercury next to the green Vega Kammback. Jay got out of the Mercury. "Need help with the trailer?" Magro said.

"Nope," Jay said, "just go ahead. Three minutes."

Magro parked the Mercury in the Post Office lot, finding a space between a chocolate-colored Porsche

911T and a Ford Country Squire. The Digger and Magro got out. Magro took the bolt cutter out of the rear seat. He held it against his body with his left arm; the rubber grips were tucked into his armpit and he cupped the short, blunt blades in his fingers.

"Nice of the government," the Digger said, "made a parking lot for the movies."

The Digger and Magro stepped through the border of the parking lot, between the low shrubs. At the sidewalk they turned left and walked down past the supermarket. In the middle of the block they waited for a blue Cadillac convertible, top down and driven by a man with a bald head, to pass. It left behind a short verse of rock music. They crossed the street and went into the alley behind the Steinman block.

The Steinman block is a four-story brick building facing Beacon Street on the south. Cabot Street is at its westerly end. The northerly side backs onto the alley; it has receiving areas for the retail stores that occupy the first floor. The building is two hundred thirty feet long, sixty feet deep at its widest point.

The Digger and Magro walked up the alley to the third receiving area. It is surrounded by a ten-foot chain-link fence equipped with a double gate. The gate was closed and padlocked.

"That Marty is a smart bastard," the Digger said. "That fuckin' fence, see? Originally the guy that owns this is gonna give Marty a key or else he's gonna leave the locks open onna gate. 'Uh uh,' Marty says, 'that'll tell 'em just like we left a note.' So he turns it down. Then I come around, he starts thinking about it, comes out here and looks. Them posts're too far apart. There's about twelve feet between them posts. Thing like this, shouldn't be more'n four, six at the most."

"Beautiful," Magro said. "How come?"

"There's a fuckin' water main under there, gas main or something. Some kind of shit. It's right near the top. They hadda spread out the posts to miss the pipes."

The Digger and Magro walked past the gates and stepped in behind the westerly fence. Cars passed on Cabot Street. The Digger and Magro stepped into the shadows. When their eyes adjusted they could see *Pavilion* in blue script on a small sign over the loading dock. The Digger knelt near the pole closest to the building wall. He took the chain-link fabric in his hands.

Magro opened the bolt cutter and started snapping the links nearest the pole. As he progressed, he and the Digger stood up. About five feet from the ground he stopped cutting.

"The other side," the Digger whispered, "come on, willya?"

Magro wiped his forehead on the back of his left glove. "Just the same as always," he whispered, "I do the fuckin' work and you bitch about it."

"I'll cut, you want," the Digger said.

Magro handed the bolt cutter to the Digger. Magro held the chain-link fabric taut against the next pole. The Digger opened the jaws of the bolt cutter their maximum inch. Then he brought the rubber grips together. He worked rapidly, the sweat breaking out on his forehead as the links popped.

"Hurry up," Magro said.

"Shut the fuck up," the Digger said. "I'm going as fast as I can."

The green Vega and the U-Haul turned into the alley in front of the supermarket as the Digger reached the five-foot mark. The Digger and Magro pushed the fabric inward and ducked under it into the receiving area. Then they turned and pushed the fabric upward, bending upward so that it hooked on the x-ends at the top of the fence.

Jay stopped the Vega and the trailer just beyond the receiving area. The Digger and Magro saw the backup lights come on. Jay swung the trailer into the receiving area next to Pavilion. He shut the lights down to parking. The Vega and the trailer moved forward. When they were straight, the backup lights came on again. Jay's head showed at the driver's side window. He backed the trailer into the Pavilion area through the hole in the fence. He cramped the wheels of the Vega and the trailer backed up to the loading dock.

Magro stepped forward and unlatched the door of the trailer. Jay got out of the car. He straddled the trailer hitch to open the rear door of the car. The Digger went to the fence. He pushed the cut section forward until the links rode off the x-ends. He lowered the cut portion slowly to the ground.

At the loading dock the Digger said, "You guys watch your ass, you get near the fence. Ends're sharper'n knives."

Magro had vaulted onto the loading platform. "Cut yourself?" Jay said. "You wanna look out, you're liable to get lockjaw from that."

"Nah," the Digger said. "Scratched myself."

"You guys having a meeting or something?" Magro said. "I try this thing or not?"

"Yeah," Jay said.

Magro stooped and grasped the handle of the overhead loading door. As he pulled, the latch snapped. The aluminum door rose silently. "Jackpot," he whispered.

The Digger and Jay clambered onto the platform. Each of them cursed. "When's the fuckin' movie get out, now?" the Digger said, breathing heavily.

Jay looked at his watch. It had a luminous dial. "Forty minutes," he said.

"We better haul ass," the Digger said.

Magro pushed the door all the way up. The only sound was the rollers on the track. "Kosher," Magro said. "No alarm switch. He didn't shit us."

They went inside. They waited until their eyes had adjusted to the deeper darkness. "Okay," the Digger said, when the racks of furs were visible. *"Let's fuckin' go,* somebody comes out of the movie early."

"Nobody leaves early," Jay said, "it's a skin flick. They got everything in it but that Great Dane you used to see all the time. They're all sitting there thinking about how they're gonna do it the same way, they get home."

The Digger and Jay each wheeled a rack to the edge of the loading platform, Magro guiding them from the front. Magro jumped to the ground. The Digger and Jay peeled the furs off the hangers and dropped them to Magro. Magro put them in the trailer.

"Take it easy," the Digger said, "throw the damned stuff around like that, Mikey-mike. That's expensive stuff."

"Animals didn't take it easy," Magro said. "Shut your

big fuckin' mouth and keep workin'." He put furs in the car.

The Digger and Jay pulled the stripped racks back into the building, the wooden handles clacking. They brought out full racks, and the wheels squeaked in the darkness. They emptied and returned all of the racks in the receiving area.

"Fine," Jay said, checking his watch. "Nineteen racks, thirty-four minutes." He jumped off the loading platform.

The Digger looked back inside once. Then he jumped heavily from the platform. Jay got into the Vega. The Digger walked toward the fence. Magro jumped lightly to the ground. He trotted to the fence behind the Digger. They rolled the fence fabric up again, but did not hook it.

Jay started the Vega. It moved forward, canted back on its rear springs. At the fence Jay said, "You got four minutes. Set off the alarm and run like a bastard."

"No running," the Digger said. "Alarm goes soon's the movie lets out. See you in Worcester."

The Vega and the trailer went through the hole in the fence. The Digger and Magro bent the wire fabric inward at waist level. When they released it, it stood slightly away from the posts. Magro picked up the bolt cutter.

The Vega and the trailer headed up the alley. The Digger and Magro saw it reach Cabot Street, hesitate and swing right.

Magro went back to the platform. He climbed up. He could see the Digger holding the corner of the wire. He could see the front of the theater on Cabot Street. He waited.

A man wearing a bright-green shirt opened the doors of the theater fully and stopped them against snubs on the sidewalk. One car went by on Cabot Street. Three women and a man emerged from the theater. The man paused and lit a cigarette. Several more people came out and lit cigarettes. A large number of people came out and the people on the sidewalk moved away. Magro could hear engines starting. He could see the Digger motionless at the fence.

Magro turned the right side of his body away from

140

the door. He allowed the bolt cutter to slip down through his left hand until he held it by one of the rubber grips. Turning his body slightly, he used a bowling motion to scale the bolt cutter noisily along the floor toward the interior door. He heard it strike, hard, and he heard the door snap open.

Magro jumped off the platform. He trotted across the pavement. The Digger went through the hole in the fence. He held it open for Magro. Together they bent the fabric back against the previous bend and tangled some of the cut ends together.

They straightened up quickly and put their hands in their pockets. At the Cabot Street end of the alley five moviegoers turned in. The Digger and Magro were back-to to the moviegoers, and about ninety yards ahead of them, when they reached the Post Office lot. Several people had reached the lot by different routes. The Digger and Magro got into the Mercury. It started at the same time as four other cars.

Magro swung the Mercury out of the lot and into the movie traffic. He turned right on Cabot Street and headed north, toward Commonwealth Avenue.

Twelve minutes after the Vega pulled out of the alley, Magro turned left on Commonwealth Avenue and proceeded at the legal limit toward the Massachusetts Turnpike. At the same time the Newton Police, hampered by the movie traffic and using no sirens, parked four prowl cars near Pavilion, two in front and two in back.

"Keep in mind, now," Sergeant Duggan said, "that's a silent alarm. There could be guys in there with guns, and they don't know we're coming. You don't get paid for getting shot."

15

THE GREEK surveyed the turquoise shag rug in Schabb's private office. Schabb sat behind a kidney-shaped birch desk; the kneehole was screened in woven cane. Torrey sat to the left in a brown Naugahyde chair, set on a chromium pedestal. There was a Panasonic pop-up television set on the desk; the telephone was in a walnut box. Two prints of Degas paintings were on the wall.

"All right," the Greek said. "I see it all."

"Just what do you think, Greek?" Schabb said.

"I tell you," the Greek said, "originally I come in here, I open the door and there's this crotch at the desk there, I was gonna say, 'Excuse me, must've got off the wrong floor.' So I take a quick look at the door, it says, 'Regent,' I gotta be inna right place, there's nothing wrong with the brain or anything. It's just, the last time I'm here, there's no tits in a see-through blouse staring me inna face when I come in."

"She's got a bra on, Greek," Torrey said.

"I know she's got a bra on," the Greek said. "I could see the fuckin' bra, don't forget. I figure we're gonna spend all this time on it, I would've read the fuckin' label. She's also got a mole on her left one, where the bra goes down, there.

"So I think to myself, Richie's gone and done it. Then I see the *rug,* and the cabinets, and I, I *don't* see you guys. So I say to Miss Tits, where are you? And she says, 'Who?' Well, them two guys, the one

142

that eats you and the one pays you money so the first one can eat you. Them guys. Your fuckin' employers."

Torrey got up and shut the door. "Greek," he said. "you really got a mouth on you like a fuckin' sewer, you know that?"

"The worst thing I ever put in my mouth was a cigar," the Greek said. "I know some guys can't say that. Now this is my money too. I gotta right to know what's going on. All of a sudden this thing I own part of gets turned into a fuckin' first-line whorehouse and nobody ever sent me no letter or nothing. How much does Miss Tits cost? That's for openers. Then we get to the rest of this shit you guys've got all of a sudden."

"That kid is Joanie Halb," Torrey said. "I know her brother, took himself a bad one down the track about four years ago, swapping spit boxes. She's a nice kid and I'm helping a guy out. Eighty-five a week and she can answer the phone and do typing. That's all she is and that's all she does."

"He's gonna eat her," the Greek said, to Schabb. "By ten fifteen today she'll blow him. And private offices too, huh? How much this cost?"

"Two eighty on paper," Schabb said. "Two sixty, actually. It was two eighty for this, they knocked the wall out. But for the two of them, five twenty."

"What about all this *shit* you got in here?" the Greek said. "Them hairy rugs, this museum shit. How much am I out on this?"

"Total?" Schabb said, hesitating and looking at Torrey.

"Total," the Greek said, "and never mind waiting for him to give you the word. I think I gotta right, know how mucha my money you assholes're throwing out the window'thout asking me."

"Around three hundred a month," Schabb said. "I'm not sure on the rugs, yet. We rent the rest of the stuff."

"That's a hundred of mine," the Greek said. He looked at Torrey. "I figure, about one eighty a month of my money this little thing of yours, you didn't even ask me. I gotta loan around a thousand and make four calls to make that. That's a nice goddamned thing to find out. You fuckin' cocksucker, I could fuckin' kill you for this."

143

"I didn't ask you," Torrey said, "because Miller suggested it and I thought it'd be a good idea and I really didn't give a shit whether you liked it or not."

The Greek sat down fast. He did not say anything. He kept his face clear of expression.

"You want a cup of coffee, Greek?" Schabb said.

"If I do," the Greek said, looking at Torrey, "I suppose I got to go out for it. I'm the nigger now, is that it?"

"Hell, no," Schabb said. "We've got the pot right up here."

"I don't want no fuckin' coffee," the Greek said.

"He drinks it black, Mill," Torrey said. "Have Joanie bring him in a cup. You'll be all right, Greek. Nothing like a nice hot cup of coffee, shape a man up. Okay for your diet, too, right? See how we're thinking about you?"

"I said," the Greek said, "I said I don't want no fuckin' coffee."

Schabb said into the intercom, "Joanie, please bring Mister Almas a black coffee, no sugar."

The girl brought the coffee. She walked primly across the rug and set the cup on the desk. She walked primly back and looked inquiringly at Torrey. He shook his head. She went out and shut the door quietly.

"Whyn't you spill it on the rug, Greek?" Torrey said. "Maybe that'd make you feel better."

"You cuntlapper," the Greek said.

"Greek," Torrey said, "have your coffee. Think about what you're doing to yourself. You got a chance here, move into the big leagues to stay. You're fucking it up. You're mucking us up. I hate to see a man, don't know what his own best interests are."

The Greek hunched forward in the chair. "You listen to me," he said. "I been around longer'n you have and I know what I'm talking about. You're the one that's gonna fuck up. I seen guys like you before, didn't know which end's their ass and which end's their fuckin' tool. You're gonna attract attention to this thing. You're gonna fuck it up, and you're gonna try to drag him and me down with you. Not me, Richie, not me. This here's partly mine. You can go out inna street and wave your dick at the cabs, you want, it don't matter to me. But my money, my money matters. Every time you spend a fuckin' buck, thirty-four cents of it's mine. Don't tell me, my best interests, I get to come in once a week and a free cup of coffee, don't gimme none of that shit. I'm the guy makes this thing go, and I'm not taking no more shit like this from you."

"Have some coffee, Greek," Torrey said.

"I don't want no fuckin' coffee," the Greek said. "You're fuckin' with me, Richie, and I know a couple guys, fucked with me, they got in trouble."

"You're right, Greek," Torrey said. "I know both of them guys and you're right. I apologize. One of them steals suits down to Robert Hall's and he can't understand it, nobody wants to buy them. I forget what the other guy's doing. I think he's stealing hubcaps offa Studebakers. Them the two guys you mean?"

The Greek turned to look to Schabb. "You with him, Mill? Is that it? You and him against me?"

"Look," Schabb said, "I'm a nice guy. I came in with a guy that knows junkets and a guy that knows how to collect. I thought this was just about what I was looking for. I thought it was just business. Turns out, it isn't. I'd like somebody to tell me what kind of game we're playing. Then I'll pick sides, if I have to."

"I can kick the shit out of you, you know, Mister Schabb," the Greek said. "It won't cost me no more, kick the shit outa you along with him. You keeping that in mind?"

"Greek," Schabb said, leaning back in the chair, "I calculate that there's about four million people who can kick the shit out of me. So far, nobody has. You know why?"

The Greek did not answer.

Schabb clasped his hands behind his head. "Nobody kicked the shit out of me," he said, "because I always look around very carefully before I do anything. And when I see a fellow, looks as though he might kick the shit out of me, I avoid him. I don't think I'd like what he might have in mind."

"Well," the Greek said, "how's your vision now?"

"Pretty good," Schabb said. "I shaved this morning and I didn't cut myself."

"Good," the Greek said. "Now, me and Richie,

we've sort of got you where one of us is probably gonna kick the shit out of you. So which way you gonna flop?"

"Out," Schabb said.

"Out?" the Greek said, looking at Torrey. "Out where? Ain't no out. There's me and there's Richie. That is the lineup. There ain't no out."

"There is for me," Schabb said.

"Lemme hear about it," the Greek said. "I'm generally pretty good at seeing outs. Where is it?"

"Well," Schabb said, "you guys seem to be running a pissing contest here, right?" Neither the Greek nor Torrey answered. "Right," Schabb said, "that's what I thought. And it's over the business. Now, what's the business?"

"Junkets and sharking," the Greek said.

"Nope," Schabb said. "That's what the business was before we started all these things. Richie had the junkets, you had the, well, lending business. That's not this business. This business is the rugs and the prints and the girl and the files and the brochure. It's the investment in the Holy Name tour. *This* business is me, fronting for you guys."

"I'm still listening," the Greek said.

"You better listen pretty close," Torrey said. "That's Mill's polite way of telling you, he's the business. He can do without us, mostly."

"Miller's getting a little fat for my taste," the Greek said. "Maybe I'm fighting the wrong guy." To Schabb he said, "You're saying you're gonna run it, that it?"

"Nope," Schabb said. "I'm telling you, I know how to run something that's different'n anything either one of you guys knows about. I can run it for you guys, because I need you guys, or I can run it for somebody else. Doesn't matter to me. But I can tell you one thing, Greek: I'm not fighting anybody for it. Because all I have to do is leave, and I take this business with me, and you and Richie can beat each other shitless. It won't matter a bit to me. I'm going to make this thing a genuine business. Those file cabinets, when I get them working, will give me a reliable list of guys who play hard and lose respectable amounts of money and pay up afterwards. Everything."

"I keep that in my head," the Greek said.

"I keep shit in my ass," Torrey said. "Listen to the man for a change, willya? You really want to be chickenshit all your life? He knows something we don't."

"I could take you apart right here, you know," the Greek said to Richie.

"You could get shot right here, too," Richie said.

"You got a lot of cheap talk," the Greek said.

"Depends on who's getting the bill," Torrey said. "I know a couple guys too, you know."

"Now that's what I mean," Schabb said. "I've got better things to do'n listen to you guys fight over bones. I think you're a couple of assholes. You're worse'n guys that sell stock. They spend all their time getting laid and drunk, no time for business. You guys fight all the time, no time for business. Two weeks from now, Greek, I can get by without either one of you. Six months from now, unless something happens that I sure can't see, I can run it better all by myself. Those're facts, Greek. So, you ask me who I'm with, I'm against both of you. You're just an annoyance to me. Especially you. Richie's at least creative enough to see what I can do."

"And in the meantime," the Greek said, "inna meantime I go a third of Richie's private office cunt. And your fuckin' rugs and stuff. I'm the one that's gotta go down to Dorchester there, nobody ever asks me what I think, you fuck up my regular business, and six months from now I'm just supposed to pack out."

"No," Schabb said. "Six months from now you've got a third of a very going concern. All you got to do in the meantime is let somebody do things you're not used to seeing done. Take a few risks, Greek. You could end up a respectable businessman."

"You got any idea how you piss me off?" the Greek said.

"He doesn't give a shit, Greek," Torrey said.

The Greek looked at Schabb.

"I don't give a shit either," Torrey said. "I told him that. He's not with me, Greek. I'm with him."

The Greek stared at each of them. "Lemme tell you something, Mister Schabb," he said. "One of them great guys of yours, lives out to Dover, went to Vegas?

Lost himself seven. I go around and see him, he said he wasn't gonna *pay*. 'Gambling debts're uncollectible in Massachusetts,' he says. I said, 'Whaddaya mean? What is this shit?' He says, 'Go ahead and sue me. I talked to my lawyer. See how far you get.'

"I look at him," the Greek said. "I said, 'Mister, I guess you probably don't know much. I'm not suing you. I don't sue nobody. *Fuck* suing. I been collecting money twenty years now. I never sued anybody in my life. That's not the way it works.'

"So he says, 'Well, I'm not paying, otherwise.' I said, 'Yes you are. You just don't know it yet. You're gonna pay. You're gonna pay every fuckin' dime.'

"He gets this little smile on his puss," the Greek said. "See, I'm in his office, just like I'm in yours now, I'm used to that, I see that little kind of grin there, I know what's going on. He's got the Dictaphone on. Tryin' to suck me in. 'Are you threatening me, sir?' he says, the asshole, thinks he can blow one by me like that. I say, 'Look, sir, my advice to you, you go right down the FBI and you tell them everything I said. Only, I advise you, don't tell them nothing I didn't say, because I got a thing on me that puts everything I said to you on a tape I got down in the trunk of my car, and you tell them I said something I didn't say, I'm gonna play that tape back and they can prosecute you for that.' He don't smile so much then. I say, 'Them fellas the experts. You ask them, am I threatening you or not. Get it all off your chest. Then get the goddamned money up, all right?' "

"So?" Torrey said.

"This morning," the Greek said, "I got a nice little check from that guy in Dover. Made out to cash, just like it's supposed to be. And it's good. I can tell by feeling it. And the next week and the week after. I don't think I'm gonna have to sue him after all."

"Uh huh," Schabb said.

"You oughta think about that, Mister Schabb," the Greek said, "about just what you got here, with Richie to help you. Richie's just like the FBI. He's good now, but inna middle of the night you can't always get to him fast when you need him. I knew a guy, more'n one, goes bellyaching to the cops when somebody comes around to collect what he owes, they give him all kinds of stuff, they'll protect him, he don't have nothing to worry about. Then they go home and have dinner, and they go on vacation and all, and the next thing you know, somebody comes around when he don't expect it and kind of run him up against a wall a few times, break his nose and some teeth and stuff, and he turns up with kidney trouble. I advise you, Mister Schabb, you think about just where you are, and then you call me. I'll give you a little time. I don't want to be unreasonable with a partner, you know?"

The Greek stood up. He stared at Schabb and he hitched up his pants.

"I'll give it some thought," Schabb said.

The Greek nodded. He stepped to the door and opened it. He turned to look at Torrey. "I'm not finished with you yet either, Richie," he said. "I gotta think what I'm gonna do with you. I don't like trouble. Trouble makes heat, and heat's bad for business, and I don't like that. But I think probably, you and me got something we're probably gonna have to settle out, one way, the other."

"Your convenience," Torrey said.

The Greek left the room. He did not close the door. He walked past Joanie Halb without saying anything. He opened the outer door and went out and closed the door behind him.

Torrey leaned back when the other door closed. "Now lemme ask you," he said, "you still think there's a way, get along with that guy?"

"No way in the world," Schabb said.

"So that leaves what I been thinking about," Torrey said. "You got any idea what that is?"

"Yeah," Schabb said.

"You got any objections?" Torrey said.

"Nope," Schabb said. "Somebody doesn't do something to him, I got his promise he'll do something to me. That cuts down on the objections, fast."

"You gonna help?" Torrey said.

"Yeah," Schabb said.

"It's gonna be early inna morning," Torrey said.

"Look," Schabb said, "I'd rather it was him early in the morning, me late at night."

149

16

IN THE AFTERNOON Harrington inquired about the possibility of another job.

"Jesus," the Digger said, "you're like one of them cheerleaders in high school, got a taste of the dog and now you can't leave it alone."

"I was looking at boats," Harrington said. "The two'll buy a nice one. But no dock and all, I'm gonna have to tow it. For that I need a new car. I'll rip the transmission right out of the Ford, I pull a boat with it. I was just wondering."

"My friend," the Digger said, "you get a gaff job like that once in a lifetime. Another one comes along, though, I'll tell you. Hell, I'll give this place back to Evvie Malloy and she can give it back to O'Dell, all I care. I could get one of them a month, I'd sleep till noon every day."

"Sure," Harrington said. "Well, I was just wondering. See, I was reading the *Record* today and all."

"That's what I kind of thought," the Digger said. "I figured that was it."

"I didn't mean nothing, Dig," Harrington said. "I was just saying."

"You seen the reward ad," the Digger said.

"It was kind of hard not to," Harrington said. "Twenty-five thousand and all, that insurance company."

"You should've tried harder, my friend," the Digger said.

"Well," Harrington said, "thing made it hard, was, I see where that stuff's worth about two hundred thousand."

"That's about double, as usual," the Digger said.

"Okay," Harrington said, "but still, I got two for what I did."

"That's what you agreed to," the Digger said. "You're a fuckin' beauty about it, too, the thing was going on. You're scared shitless."

"I was," Harrington said. "Now, now I think I done what I did too cheap. You and Marty and Mikey-mike must've got about thirty-five apiece."

The Digger leaned on the bar. "Lemme tell you something, Harrington," he said, "you take the rough with the fuckin' smooth in this life. I went out to Vegas there and I said, 'Fuck me, fuck me.' And they fucked me. Then I get that gaff job. I got *un*fucked. Mikey-mike made some dough. Marty made some dough. I made some dough. You even made some dough, and it come right out of the sky for you, my friend. I'm okay with the wife again, everything's all right."

The Digger straightened up again. "Now one thing I like," he said, "I like everything all right. I don't like the wife pissed off. I like going home, she's all happy because we're going San Juan. I like it, I got Bloom paid off. I feel good. Feels good to feel good. I missed it. I wouldn't like it, somebody was to get me fucked up again."

"Well," Harrington said, "I know. But I don't like it, I got taken advantage of." He drank his beer.

"Ah," the Digger said, "I took advantage. I paid you two for driving. I get a cabbie any night I want, take me into deepest darkest Roxbury for that, my friend. Now you take some advice: you go buy your boat. And you forget about the car. And you keep your fuckin' mouth shut, understand? You could wind up dead, you know."

Harrington finished his beer. He did not meet the Digger's eyes. Without looking up he said, "I'm going home now." He slid off the stool.

17

"I SHOULD'VE HAD BREAKFAST," Schabb said. He held the Impala with the brake at the intersection of Madison Street and the Southern Artery in Quincy. The car surged periodically. The traffic light remained red. It was six-ten in the morning. The gas stations and the automobile dealerships were quiet in the morning light.

"You oughta get this thing looked at," Torrey said. "Fuckin' thing's lunging. Idle's too high."

"I hadda guy look at it," Schabb said. "Every time I cramp the wheels, the power steering stalls it out. When I start it, cold, she stalls. So he fixed it. Now it creeps. I dunno."

"You had an asshole look at it," Torrey said. The light changed. The Impala moved forward. "He looked at it and he didn't know what was wrong with it. So, he set the idle up. You're wearing out the brakes and the fuckin' rear end. What you needed was a fuckin' tune-up, somebody knew how to do a fuckin' tune-up."

"He said something about the pollution thing," Schabb said. The car moved south on the Southern Artery.

"They're all doing that now," Torrey said. "That's the big excuse for guys, don't know what they're doing. They oughta build that guy Nader a fuckin' monument, what he did for dumb mechanics."

"This guy's always been all right with me," Schabb

152

said. "I've been doing business with him a long time. He kept the Cad running all right."

"That's another way of saying," Torrey said, "he's been fucking you a long time. Somebody did to me what he did to you, I'd let him do it once. Then I'd go back, it still didn't run right, I'd give him a couple shots."

The clam stands and the liquor stores were dark along the Artery. "I could still use breakfast," Schabb said. "I haven't been up this early since I took the kid fishing. All I had was coffee, and only about half a cup of that."

"Look," Torrey said, "there's a Dunkin' Donuts up here at the intersection, way I remember it."

"Okay," Schabb said. They passed a fuel oil depot on the left and a Volkswagen dealership on the right.

"But you're not stopping there," Torrey said. "You're turning right, there. Then we're gonna do what we came to do, and then you're going back and drop me off, and then you can go home and have a fuckin' jelly doughnut if you want. Nobody writes down no numbers today."

"I am fuckin' *starved,*" Schabb said.

"You are fuckin' *scared,*" Torrey said. "I don't blame you. This's your first run. Everybody's scared on the first run. Everybody wants to stop and eat. Anything to put it off. Take a shit, anything. Just so you don't have to do it."

"Richie," Schabb said, "I'm not kidding. I really am hungry."

"I know that," Torrey said. "I didn't say you're making it up. My first time, I was convinced, I hadda take a shit. I told them. I was nineteen fuckin' years old, you should've heard all the shit I took, I said I hadda take a shit. They wouldn't let me. So I whack a guy out, practically in Scollay Square, the guy that was supposed to do it was sick and I hadda do it, I took him out nice and clean. And I shit myself.

"They started calling me 'Shitpants,' " Torrey said. "But then, I was twenty-two, I got a contract on one of the guys made a lot of fun of me. I see him coming out of the place and he sees me and I'm getting out of the car with the piece and he says, 'No, no,

153

Richie, look, I'll straighten it out.' And I just look at him and I keep coming at him and he's got his hands up. He says, his hands're up like he's trying to give me something, he says, 'No, Richie, look, gimme a little time.' I say, 'What're you calling me Richie for? How come you're not calling me Shitpants?' Then I gutshoot him. Then I gutshot him again. He puts the hands down. Ever kick a man inna balls?"

"No," Schabb said. "I hit a guy in the teeth once, but he was grabbing my wife's ass at a party and I more or less had to."

"No," Torrey said. "Well, you gutshoot a guy and it hits him, he grabs just like a guy that's grabbing for the balls, that you kicked inna balls. Like he's worried, he's gonna lose them.

"Guy does the same thing," Torrey said, "you shoot him inna belly with a thirty-eight. It's just slow enough so he can still stand up. Forty-five'd knock him over. He gets them hands right over the holes and he holds on.

"This guy looked down," Torrey said, "sees the blood on his nice grey suit, running out his fingers. Looks up again.' 'Lemme alone, Richie,' he says, 'lemme alone. I can straighten it out.'

" 'Call me Shitpants,' I say, and by now I'm right on top of him, and he actually kneels down. I got the piece pointing right practically in his eye. 'Lemme alone, Richie,' he says, he's still got his hands on his belly, his head's way back on his neck.

" 'Still calling me Richie,' I say, 'how come you're not calling me Shitpants, huh?" Then I say, 'Here comes the rest.' He was hurting. His mouth's going, nothing comes out. I shot him in the face."

"Jesus," Schabb said.

"You shot a man inna face," Torrey said, "close range, it kinda of comes apart, you know? All flies to pieces, bone chips and stuff."

"Cut it out," Schabb said. The car slowed at the linoleum store and stopped at the light.

"He shit himself," Torrey said. "Man dies, every thing lets go. You could smell it. About two seconds after I shoot him in the face, I shoot him again, and he goes right over backwards and you could hear everything letting go. Smell it too, like I say."

"Okay, Richie," Schabb said, "you did it. I'm not hungry any more."

"Hell," Torrey said, "that wasn't why I told you. Makes me sick too. That's the last hit I had. Guy called me in, next one come up. Them things don't pay bad, you know? Says, 'Maybe you wonder why we didn't use you.' I said, 'No.' He says, 'Well, the last time, we heard you liked it too much. That's why.' Get that? I was actually very scared. It's natural to be scared. I'm scared now. It was just, there was something personal in that one, I didn't tell them guys about. This one, there's nothing personal, so I don't have nothing else. I can feel scared, I can think about it. But, being scared, it's natural. Just like the first time you get laid. Always decide, I want a turkey dinner, soup and salad and dessert and nuts. It's just a way, putting it off, you don't have to face it so soon.

"The thing you got to understand," Torrey said, "is that you have gotta face it. Me, I'd much rather stop and have a couple doughnuts and we let the Greek get down the gym and then there's too many people around and we go home, do it tomorrow. But then you just gotta be scared all over again tomorrow. Don't do any good. Turn right."

The car took the right and proceeded a hundred yards past a Dunkin' Donuts stand. There were two trailer trucks parked at the street. Inside, at the counter, slope-shouldered men bent over magenta cups, filled with coffee.

"Turn right again," Torrey said. Schabb turned off Route Three-A onto Weymouth Street.

Weymouth Street was crowded with double-decker houses painted brown and ivory, white and green, and grey and white. Each house had a first-floor front porch and a second-floor front porch. The second-floor porches were crowded with charcoal grills and tricyles and aluminum mesh chairs. The first-floor porches were empty. There were no lights on.

"Go up about six houses and pull over," Torrey said.

Schabb parked under the overhanging branches of a maple tree.

"Turn the radio on," Torrey said.

"Turn it on yourself," Schabb said.

"Look," Torrey said, "don't be any more of a pain in the ass than you gotta be, all right?"

"I'm not the nigger any more," Schabb said.

"Oh Christ," Torrey said. He turned the radio on.

"What're you listening for anyway?" Schabb said.

"I'm not listening for anything," Torrey said. "I just want the fuckin' radio on, all right?"

"It's all right with me," Schabb said. "What're you getting so jumpy about?"

"Shut off the fuckin' engine," Torrey said.

The Impala whispered down beneath the tree. It was twenty minutes past six.

"All right," Torrey said, as the radio gave the extended weather forecast, "see the green and white up on the left, maroon Bird with the vinyl roof inna yard?"

"Yeah," Schabb said.

"His," Torrey said. "Y's about ten, twelve minutes from here. Opens at seven, right?"

"That's what he says," Schabb said.

"Right," Torrey said. "But the Greek's careful. He'll give himself twenny minutes. He's a slow driver, too. Maybe twenny-five minutes. He'd rather get there and sit in the car and wait, than be late. So I figure, next fifteen minutes, he comes out. Soon's I see him, you start up, we roll up and let him have it and that'll be the end of that. Okay?"

"Okay," Schabb said.

Torrey reached under his jacket with his right hand. From the area near his left kidney he withdrew a large revolver from his belt.

"What's that?" Schabb said.

"Ruger Blackhawk," Torrey said. "I was counting onna guy to get me a shotgun, he comes up with this. Probably better anyway. Greek won't see this so fast."

"Jesus," Schabb said, "minute he sees us roll up, he's gonna know. He's gotta gun himself, hasn't he?"

"Thirty-eight," Torrey said. He opened the cylinder lock, examined the cylinder and found all chambers loaded. He closed the cylinder with a snap.

"You should've got the shotgun," Schabb said.

"Look," Torrey said, "you do the best you can. Keep in mind, I'm gonna have this out. He's gonna have that thirty-eight in his pants. Thirty-eight's a two-incher. This's a four. I still got all the edge I need. Start the fuckin' car."

"What?" Schabb said.

"*Start the fuckin' car*," Torrey said. "Door's opening. That's his foot. See it?"

Schabb started the car and put it in gear.

"Let her creep," Torrey said.

Schabb saw the left side of a man's body emerge from the aluminum storm and screen door on the first-floor porch of the green-and-white house. He saw the tail of the Greek's sport coat. He saw the rest of the Greek, from the back. He saw the Greek start down the steps.

"Give her some gas," Torrey said. He had the revolver in his right hand. "Keep her onna curb, take her along."

The Impala moved down the street. It passed a brown-and-ivory double-decker, a brown-and-white double-decker, and a white-and-grey double-decker. The Greek was at the bottom of the stairs. He took a springy step onto the walk. He passed swiftly around the right rear of the Thunderbird sedan. The driveway was two strips of concrete in grass.

"Up a little," Torrey said, "fast."

Schabb nudged the accelerator. The Impala reached the place where the Greek's drive met the street.

"Stop," Torrey said.

Schabb stood on the brake and the front end of the Impala dove. Schabb heard the passenger door open. He saw Torrey's left leg leaving the car. He heard Torrey say, "Greek."

Schabb had his head around. He saw Torrey sprinting up the driveway from the street. Torry was in a semicrouch. His right arm was stiff in the upper arm. Schabb could not see the forearm.

Schabb saw the Greek crouch. He saw the Greek's right hand flash back toward his belt, then forward again with a revolver. He saw Torrey's right arm stiffen. Torrey's body was at a different angle, turned slightly away from the right. Schabb saw the Greek's hand pick up, then down.

Schabb saw Torrey reel slightly. Schabb saw the Blackhawk briefly as it pointed toward the sky. Schabb saw the Greek crouch at the left rear fender of the Bird. He saw the Greek's hand kick up with the revolver, then kick down again. He heard shots. He saw Torrey stagger back. He saw the Blackhawk pointing toward the sky. He saw the Greek's right hand kick upward again. He saw Torrey's body lurch in its stride. He saw the Greek straighten up. He heard the shot. He saw the Greek point the black revolver at Torrey, as Torrey's body recovered its balance again. The Blackhawk flew out of Torrey's hand. Schabb saw the Greek's right hand kick up, then down. Schabb saw a white piece fly away from Torrey's head, in the back. Schabb heard the shot. Schabb saw Torrey reel back again. Schabb jammed the accelerator to the floor. The motor roared wildly. Schabb jerked the transmission out of PARK. The Impala leaped forward as Torrey came down on the grass. Schabb rolled the wheel over to miss a white Plymouth Fury at the curb, one door down from the Greek's. The Impala slewed. Schabb hauled the wheel over hard. The Impala slewed to the right. Schabb got the Impala straightened out.

At the corner of the street, Schabb turned the Impala hard right. He looked back as the car turned. The Greek stood two hundred yards back. His hands were at his sides.

18

SALLY BARCA was sitting at Schabb's desk when
Schabb came into the Regent Sportsmen's Club.

"Who're you?" Schabb said. "How'd you get in
here?"

"My name's Barca," Sally said. "Come in through
the front door just like any other white man, two days
ago. Where've you been?"

"I been out of town," Schabb said. "I had business
out of town. Where's Richie?"

"Aw, come on," Barca said. "Richie's still down the
Southern Mortuary, probably. I dunno where Richie
is. I know how Richie is, though, and so do you.
Where the fuck've you been?"

"Who wants to know?" Schabb said.

"You look awful white," Barca said. "You sick?
I'm a friend of Richie's. I'm one of the guys said it
was all right for him to whack out the Greek. Didn't
turn out too good for Richie, huh?"

Schabb sat down. "Richie's dead?" he said.

"You get shot four or five times, close range,"
Barca said, "it's inclined to make you dead. Where
the fuck've you been? The Greek's been practically
crazy."

"Looking for me," Schabb said.

"Looking for you to stay away from you," Barca
said. "The Greek called me, same morning. Claims
you put Richie up to it."

"I did like hell," Schabb said.

"I know that," Barca said. "I told Richie, he oughta have a contract. He was too fuckin' cheap. Tough shit for him. Where the fuck've you been?"

"I was with Richie," Schabb said.

"No shit," Barca said. "The Greek told me that. 'I could've killed him right then and there,' he said, 'and I should've.' I know where you were. Where the hell've you been?"

"I drove intown," Schabb said. "I put the car in the Under-common garage. I got a cab over to Cambridge Street. I stopped at a packy and I bought three quarts of Beefeaters. Then I got a room at the Holiday. I been there ever since."

"Drunk," Barca said.

"No," Schabb said. "Scared. I was only drunk when I was awake. I was scared all the time. I figured the Greek was gonna kill me."

"You and the Greek oughta start a club," Barca said. "The Greek thinks you're gonna kill him."

"I would've if I knew how," Schabb said.

"Since you don't know how," Barca said, "you want a new partner?"

"You gonna kill the Greek?" Schabb said. "He's hard to kill, I can tell you that much."

"Nah," Barca said, "no more need for that. The Greek says he just wants his old business back. Nobody else ever wanted it, so it's his. Me? I'm looking for new gaff. I done this and that, just like all the other assholes, spend all their time onna phone, playing music for the FBI. Except I'm not old yet, and I'm not broken down. I got the machines and stuff, and it's all right, but shit, I want something permanent. Bobby, Bobby keeps telling me, the old man fades out, Bobby's gonna be total boss and it's the pot of gold. Bobby's just old enough, swallows all that crap. And he's a nice guy. But Bobby ain't me. So I was thinking, what's the matter, you and me run this? I know what you can do, and you know, there's certain aspects, you need a guy knows his way around. We can handle things, maybe sooner or later, we get Bloom, huh?"

"And then what?" Schabb said. "What happens after that?"

"Nothing," Barca said. "We get rich, is all. After a while, Bobby and them forget it's temporary, long's they get their cut, it's all right. They'll leave us alone. Whaddaya say? And the Greek. he'll leave us alone."

"Look," Schabb said, "when I came here, I figured I had a fifty-fifty chance of being dead. I'll take anything."

Barca came out of the chair. "Okay," he said, "that's out of the way. Now lemme go see the old man and hold his hand. Oh, by the way, you wouldn't send Richie no flowers, now?"

"Mister Barca," Schabb said, "the whole idea of Regent is, you look at it hard and you can't see Richie. No way."

19

JUST BEFORE HE LEFT the Edison plant on Friday afternoon, Harrington went to the payphone and called 742-5533. The switchboard operator said, "FBI." Harrington said he had seen an ad in the paper about a reward. The switchboard operator connected him to a man who identified himself as Special Agent Falk.

"I seen the ad in the paper," Harrington said.

"What ad, sir?" the man said.

"Twenty-five thousand dollars," Harrington said, "for them fur robbers."

"The insurance company offers that, sir," the man said.

"If I tell you," Harrington said, "I get the reward?"

"The insurance company would decide that," the agent said.

"Okay," Harrington said, "lemme tell you something, you talk to the insurance and I'll call you Monday. I got the box, all right? And the paper. How's that?"

"I don't understand," the man said.

"The guys that took the furs," Harrington said.

"Yeah," the agent said.

"They cut the fence, I read inna paper," Harrington said. "A bolt cutter?"

"Yeah," the man said.

"The bolt cutter come inna box," Harrington said.

162

"Um," the man said.

"There ain't no fingerprints on the bolt cutter," Harrington said.

"Well," the man said.

"Look," Harrington said, "they was wearing gloves. They wasn't wearing gloves, they had the paper and the box. The gloves're inna box."

"Ah," the man said.

"I got the paper and the box," Harrington said.

"Uh huh," the man said.

"You call the company," Harrington said. "I gotta think this all over. I'm gonna need some protection and all, I give you that box."

"Where can I reach you?" the man said.

"I'll call you Monday," Harrington said. He hung up.

20

The Digger got home at two thirty-five in the beginning of a late September frost. His wife met him at the door. She was a wearing a lavender satin mandarin gown; it was slit above the knee on each side, and it was tight across her breasts. The Digger had removed it two years before from a crate of goods stored temporarily in the cellar of the Bright Red.

"Paul's here," she whispered.

"Oh," the Digger said, "I didn't know that. I see the big car inna street and I figured probably the Governor stopped by for a taste."

"He's been here since *midnight*," she said.

"They changed the closing hours," the Digger said. "I kept meaning to tell him."

"Jerry," she said.

"Jerry nothing," the Digger said. "I bet he enjoyed himself, looking at you in that."

"I thought you liked this," she said.

"You know goddamned right well I like that," the Digger said. "I like what you're wearing it over, too. I can see your goddamned nipples right through that stuff, for Christ sake. That's why the hell I bought it for you in the first place. Doesn't mean I want you wearing it to the fights with me, for Christ sake."

"I was wearing it for you," she said, "I was watching television and waiting for you to come home. I didn't know he was coming over."

164

"You could've changed when you found out who it was," the Digger said.

"Jerry," she said, "I would've been embarrassed. He would've known right off, it'd be like *telling* him. Besides, he's a priest."

"He's my brother, too," the Digger said. "They don't cut off your goddamned equipment when you put the collar on, you know. You give him a drink, I assume?"

"Yes," she said.

"You maybe even had a couple of pops yourself," the Digger said.

"One or two," she said.

"Good," he said, "I'll give him about, say, twenny minutes and then I'll be up and we'll do it a few times, how'll that be?"

"Best offer I had tonight," she said.

The Digger slapped his wife on the buttocks as she started up the stairs.

Paul sat in the living room. He was wearing the Roman collar and the dickey. He had removed his coat.

"An unexpected pleasure, Big Brother," the Digger said. "I get home at two in the morning, ordinarily I don't expect I'm gonna find a priest on the couch. You guys started making house calls?"

"Jerry," Paul said, "I've got one or two things on my mind, and I'm rather concerned about them. I thought maybe you could help me out."

"Well, I tell you what," the Digger said, "you just let me get myself about three ounces of something and I'll see what I can do."

The Digger returned with a glass of Jack Daniel's and ice. He sat down. "What is it, my son?" he said.

"I'll come right to the point," Paul said. "This afternoon I called up to see why it was taking so long to get my passport renewed, and after a lot of hemming and hawing I reached somebody who told me that it had been renewed but then it wasn't sent. So naturally I inquired why it wasn't sent, and when they intended to send it, and I explained about the Fahey trip, and they just wouldn't tell me. So at long last they told me to call the FBI."

"Good gracious," the Digger said, "you been burning draft cards or something, Paul baby?"

"I called the FBI," Paul said, "and I talked to a number of very polite people, and they very courteously told me almost nothing either. I began to get a little upset. I mentioned calling the Bishop and I may have even said something about the Pope. I just couldn't understand why my passport was being held up. They finally told me to call somebody in the office of the United States Attorney.

"I did that," Paul said. "I asked the man quite bluntly if the government had some reason for not wanting me to leave the country, and he was as puzzled as I was. But he said he'd look into it.

"Just before supper," Paul said, "he called me back. It seems there'd been a mistake, and he said it'd all been straightened out. I asked him, of course, what the mistake was, and he wouldn't tell me."

"But you're gonna get the passport," the Digger said.

"I expect it in the mail this week," Paul said.

"So there you are," the Digger said. "You're all set."

"Not exactly," Paul said. "I've been puzzled about that mistake all day. Then I remembered that the old passport was issued to me at the house, because I was still moving around when I got that and I wasn't sure I'd be at Holy Sepulchre permanently. And that started me thinking. I wondered if perhaps that accounted for the mistake. Maybe there was somebody else named Doherty who used to live at 58 Pershing Street who interested the government."

"Not Maureen," the Digger said, "she been hanging around with them Berrigans?"

"I doubt it," Paul said, "and probably not Kathy, either. Ma and Pa're both dead. That leaves you and me."

"Seems to," the Digger said.

"This evening I called some people I know," Paul said. "I didn't make an awful lot of progress. But I did find out that when the FBI or someone has an important investigation going on, they alert the State Department. Apparently they have some sort of a liaison office or something. Did you know that?"

166

"No," the Digger said, "it, I never really thought about it."

"No," Paul said, "well, tell me this: is there an investigation going on?"

"I suppose so," the Digger said, "them guys're generally out scouting around for something to do."

"Yes," Paul said. "Well, that was what I came over here to talk to you about. And when I got here, Aggie told me about your trip."

"Well," the Digger said, "yeah, but you don't need, we're going San Juan and all, I got the tickets today. El San Juan. But I didn't apply for no passport. You don't need any passport to go to San Juan, Puerto Rico."

"There's something you do need, though," Paul said. "You need money."

"Right," the Digger said.

"Now it wasn't so long ago," Paul said, "you came out to see me, and you were in very much the same kind of bewilderment then that I'm in tonight. You needed money, quite a lot of money, and you didn't know where you were going to get that money if I didn't give it to you."

"I remember that," the Digger said.

"I believed you," Paul said, "I believed you and I gave you some money."

"Three K," the Digger said. "Don't think I didn't appreciate it."

"And you gave something to me in exchange," Paul said, "you gave me your word that you wouldn't commit any crimes. Didn't you?"

"Yup," the Digger said.

"Now the way I look at things," Paul said, "you either lied to me or you've broken your word. Either you didn't need money, and you said you did just to cheat me, or else you did need money and you got money by committing a crime, which means you've broken your word."

"I could've mortgaged the house and stuff, like you said," the Digger said.

"You could have," Paul said. "Keeping in mind that I can call Gerry Fitz at the Registry of Deeds and find out, did you?"

"No," the Digger said.

"No," Paul said. "Now, I'm not going to ask you what you did since you talked to me, that you swore to me you wouldn't do, that's got the FBI or somebody in a mood to keep all Dohertys in the country for a while. Mostly because I'm afraid you'd tell me. You didn't kill anybody, did you?"

"No," the Digger said.

"Of course we now have a new problem," Paul said. "I don't think you lied to me when you came for the money, but I'm pretty sure you broke your word after you gave it to me, and that means you're probably willing to lie to me now, to cover what you did. So perhaps you did kill a man."

"No," the Digger said, "I didn't kill anybody."

Paul stood up. "I hope that, at least, is the truth," he said. He put on his coat. He extended his hand as the Digger got up. They shook hands. "Sit back down and finish your drink," Paul said. "I know where the door is and I can find my own way out. I just want you to know, this is the last time I'll have to do it. And you stay away from me, is that clear? You've got a good wife and a good family, and you don't know what to make of it, but there's nothing more I can do for you and there hasn't been for some time, but now I know it. And I do know it, too, is that clear?"

"Clear," the Digger said. "Good night, Paul."

Paul released his hand. "Yeah," he said, "and good night to the Digger too."

In the bedroom Agatha Doherty was reading, her back against the headboard of the bed, her legs bent to form the rest for the magazine. When the Digger came up she put down the magazine and got up and went into the bathroom. He could hear her brushing her teeth. When she emerged he looked at her and said, "You took your nightgown off."

"I did?" she said.

"I can see the nipples better now," he said, "and the hair, too. You be sure and bring that kimono to Puerto Rico."

"I'm looking forward to that," she said. She was removing the gown.

"So'm I," he said. "I got the tickets today. A-number-one, first cabin all the way. It's all set with the Magros, incidentally. He said what they'd do, they'd come over here and stay with the kids, 'stead of them going over there."

"I thought you were going to ask Harrington," she said.

"I was," the Digger said, "but Harringtons've got kids of their own, and that'd mean we'd have to take theirs. Besides, I'm never too sure what Harrington's doing." He got into bed.

"What'd Paul want?" she said, moving toward him.

"Well," the Digger said, "it's kind of a long story. Basically, I borrowed some dough off him a long time ago, and now he finds out we're finally getting a vacation and he's pissed off."

"Can't you pay him?" she said. "Or doesn't he want that?"

"Look," the Digger said, "let's kind of forget what Paul wants for a while, all right? There's something I want."

"If it's all right with you," she said, "it's all right with me."

A NOTE ABOUT THE AUTHOR

George V. Higgins is an Assistant U.S. Attorney for the District of Massachusetts. He was graduated from Boston College in 1961 and received an M.A. in English from Stanford University. He was a reporter for the Providence *Journal* and the Associated Press before obtaining a law degree from Boston College Law School in 1967. For three years he was a lawyer in the Massachusetts Attorney General's Office, in the Organized Crime Section and the Criminal Division. His first novel, *The Friends of Eddie Coyle* (1972), was a national bestseller. He lives with his wife and two children in Hingham, Massachusetts.

Bestsellers from BALLANTINE

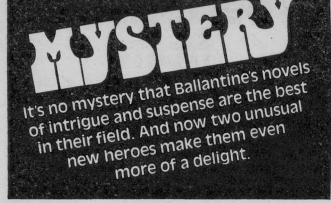